IMAGINE A DEATH

"Like a funereal mask studded w... gemstones on its inside, *Imagine a Death* embodies a vast, preternatural and intensely intimate terrain, slipping headfirst into the impossible expanses between suffering and mourning, seeking and failing, spiral and flame. For Janice Lee is not the sort to turn her back where others duck and cover; sentence by sentence, her rhapsodic fearlessness and tender logic not only reflects and withstands, it listens back; it redefines as it rewires what's gone missing; it refuses to give in to its regrets. The result is the greatest work to-date of one of America's most elemental voices and death-defiers, a kind of lamp that breaks the dark."

— **Blake Butler, author of** *Alice Knott: A Novel*

"A delicate constellation of lives both human and not that keep threatening to come together to form meaning but then, with each new section, changes shape, continuing to open up. *Imagine a Death* is an illuminating exploration of radical intersubjectivity, the understanding that even though everyone and everything potentially can touch everything else, nothing accumulates with narrative neatness. Through brilliantly complex sentences, Lee offers a disjunctive synthesis on the multifold possibilities and fears of being.

— **Brian Evenson, author of** *Song for the Unraveling of the World*

i

Imagine a Death is a roving vision quest and a blueprint for a liberational politics of being in the world. Manifold transformation occurs as shifts in consciousness disrupt patterns of traumatic encounter. Unfolding intimacies among diverse relations cause the world to flex exponentially dissolving barriers of interdependence. Intricately sensitive and lucidly aware of the urgency of attending to and engendering the flourishing of livable worlds in uncertain times, Janice Lee demonstrates how a togetherness in sentience is extended, intensified and strengthened. *Imagine a Death* is ecstatic, gorgeous and wise; a revelatory book holding the persistent glow of terrestrial reality that involves all floral, faunal and mineral presence."

— **Brenda Iijima, author of**
Remembering Animals

"In the early hours of Janice Lee's *Imagine a Death* a story is told about a crack in a wall out of which emanates an eerie light, then strange whirling sounds like eternity being shredded apart. What happens next is terrifying and profound, and seems to be not only an analogue for Lee's book, but a description of how she receives the horror vacui of the world and transforms it into a form of reparative spell-binding. *Imagine a Death* confirms Lee as the descendant of Béla Tarr, of moss that breathes, then hibernates, then breathes, of spiders in the corners of houses, of ancestral museums that only open past midnight, and of the earliest forms of shamanic storytelling."

— **Brandon Shimoda, author of**
The Grave on the Wall

"When you read Janice Lee, remember to breathe. But even if you manage to exhale, don't be too shocked to watch your breath crawl out of your mouth, unfurling like an antennaed pill-millipede successfully coaxed out of its privacy. *Imagine A Death* digs its fingernails beneath the craggy concrete slab of the ordinary and unveils a microcosmos of alien critters, teeming with perverse life of all kind . . . feelings and observations so subtle you wonder how they fell into [Lee's] trap. Read this story of trauma and connection and feeling and dreams and world endings. Read especially now during a pandemic apocalypse. Let [*Imagine a Death*] lure you into a breathless consideration: that the apocalypse isn't so much about cataclysmic endings as it is about the spritely appearing of a hue of a colour not yet named, of a connection newly made, of a howl sublimated into a sky that holds all things."

— **Bayo Akomolafe, author of** *These Wilds Beyond Our Fences: Letters to My Daughter on Humanity's Search for Home*

"It swarms, it engulfs, it burns with fabulous agglutination, it is a doorway to the other planes. The language rivets. Not unlike Egyptian psychology its protracted density can cause nutation in the cellular structure itself. The impact of evolutionary activism."

— **Will Alexander, author of** *The Sri Lankan Loxodrome* **and** *Compression & Purity*

IMAGINE
A
DEATH

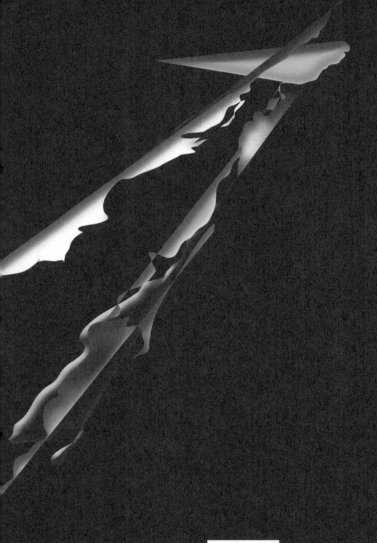

INNOVATIVE PROSE SERIES

Series Editor: Katie Jean Shinkle

texasreviewpress.org
Huntsville • Texas

IMAGINE A DEATH

JANICE LEE

A NOVEL

.trp

www.texasreviewpress.org
Huntsville, Texas 77341

Library of Congress Cataloging-in-Publication Data
Lee, Janice, author
Imagine a death : a novel / Janice Lee.
Other titles: Innovative prose series
Description: Huntsville : Texas Review Press, [2021]
LCCN 2021017000 (print) | LCCN 2021017001 (ebook)
ISBN 9781680032550 (paperback)
ISBN 9781680032567 (ebook)

Subjects: LCSH: Death--Psychological aspects--Fiction. | Psychic
trauma--Fiction. | Traumatic incident reduction--Fiction. |
Mental healing--Fiction. | LCGFT: Novels.
Classification: LCC PS3612.E342945 I43 2021 (print)
LCC PS3612.E342945 (ebook)
DDC 813/.6--dc23
LC record available at https://lccn.loc.gov/2021017000
LC ebook record available at https://lccn.loc.gov/2021017001

Cover Design: Bradley Alan Ivey
Book Design/Graphics: PJ Carlisle

What really exists is not things made but things in the making.
— **William James,** *A Pluralistic Universe*

We are all contemplatives of an ongoing apocalypse.
— **Etel Adnan,** *Master of the Eclipse*

CONTENTS

1. THE WRITER

Imagine a death, which really occurs—that is, not the
death which devastates inside a dream as you sleep,
the kind of dream from which you wake up sweating,
the gray sheets dampened and the room suddenly filled
with the cold sweat of someone who has been asleep
for an intolerable amount of time, alone in the dark,
the kind of dream in which you wake up and want to
call your brother to see if he is still breathing, *Are you
alive?* you want to ask, knowing that the answer is yes
and knowing he is home in his bed dreaming his own
dream of wanting to occupy another body that is not
his own, dreaming of his mother, of when she was
alive, and you recall the particular dreams you have of
a mother that are different than his dreams of the same
woman, and when you are awake you imagine all the
cold and hard touches of a love buried, then excavated
violently from the foul-smelling earth, the grappling,
bloodied body of your dream, the imagined death of a
loved one that is so common on these sleepless nights
when it is easier to dream of death rather than life
and when the imagined deaths of movies are so easy
to digest, as the scene of the decapitation of a lovely
maiden, the close-up of her neck, the careful removal
of her necklace, this fictitious and choreographed
scene that is designed to induce tears and empathy,
and without fail you are bawling and imagining the
suffering of a girl who is only sixteen and of those who

1

have dared to love her and you can't feel the warmth
leaving her body but you *can* imagine the anticipation
of the quick death that awaits her, the slight itch on
her nose that can't help but become an afterthought
in the moment before a death when she does not want
to spend the last few seconds of life scratching her
nose, her hands bound behind her, her lips pursed
and waiting, the graceful trail of blood that leads away
from the scene—no, not a death like that, but a death
that really occurs outside the window at night, the
sitting tensely in the dark listening to the irregular
noises of animals that signal pain and fright and injury,
the screeching of a cat out there in the bushes, quick
scurries in the dark and frantic confusion, and she
might try to stir herself out of bed and put on pants
before slipping outside barefoot in an attempt to track
the source of the cursed creature, in an attempt to
do something, to at least witness the event, whatever
the event might be, though the now too-long silence
seems to indicate quite clearly the circumstances of
the event itself and she already knows how this ends,
how it always ends, and if she has heard the scream,
it has occurred already and if there is now silence, it
has occurred already, and if she is starting to feel that
tightening in her chest, it has occurred already, and if
she doesn't close her eyes now, it has occurred already,
and right now she can't handle that kind of heartbreak,
not when she has been trying to fall asleep for hours
and though she can blame the sleeplessness on the
noises outside and though she has managed to doze
off for a few moments at a time, she has only dreamed
of death, which perhaps is still more of a relief than to
dream of sitting at home in front of a fire that warms
and gives the false picture of an elusive peace and the
ghastly kind of contentment that terrifies husbands
into running away from their wives, that asks children

to forgive the repeated abuses of their parents, that convinces fish that the confines of their tanks are the borders of the world and the edges of their universe, and while she lies awake she finds herself constantly swatting away the moths that circle and build like a gradually growing swarm, building up on the walls and windows and lamps of her room and she finds them drawn to her face illuminated by the moonlight coming in through the window, the brown moths clinging to her cheek when she is sleeping and she thinks, *there has been enough death for one night;* she has already had to smoosh seventeen moths with a tissue and flush them down the toilet so there is no chance of them coming back as ghosts to enact their revenge and haunt her for her offenses against their species but also to hide any evidence of the fact that she has had to kill so many moths in recent nights and though she believes that she has no moral objection to killing the flying creatures that disturb her immensely, she is afraid of the potential consequences of killing these symbolic winged things and also of sleeping under a full moon when the sky is so full of ash and her heart is so full of provisional drowning, for she will, after all, be judged only for her actions in the end and not the tangential tinges of guilt or shame that accompany any of them, her fingers squeezing each other and her eyes, wet and open, in the pitiable darkness.

Currently her heart is the size of a grapefruit, beating softly then thumping like a jackhammer, the sour juice being squeezed out into the rest of her body and she dreams of sleep or sleeps of dreams; it's hard to know the difference when the shadows cast on the walls by the trees outside only magnify the sensation of being eaten alive by moths and she can't stop imagining possibilities and alternate possibilities.

Imagine the sky, which holds things. Even the dog that just lies there, limp and frightened, knows generally that the sky *can* hold things and that on some days the sky might be lighter and emptier, and that on other days it might be filled and penetrated with an unpredictable continuation of history and love and fire. He whimpers softly but she does not hear him, for she has managed, at least for a moment, to find respite through the relief of unconsciousness as the pea vines outside creep up the wall, find each other, find the wall again, and continue their steady growth, the sensitivity of plants as regular and bold as the dog's breath, his nose on the floor, slight particles of dirt lifted upward slightly off the floor from the air moving around them.

It was now the next night, or the night after that, and she lay there again in the familiar, ill-fitting position of restless body, eyes open, leering at the ceiling's coarseness and recalled that inside a dream she had made the decision to open the front door but couldn't remember when she had been asleep long enough to dream such a mundane action, and if it were a memory, she felt doubly perplexed at who she would have allowed into her home at this hour. She was washing her hands now because that is what one did when one's hands were dirty and she washed her hands under the hot water, eyes about to burst open from the intense gaze she had been wearing for so many moments and she washed her hands because that is what one did when their hands were dirty and her hands were dirty now. Under the hot water, she washed her hands, furiously wringing and clasping her hands, scrubbing her palms with her nails, intent and watching the blood spiral away from her, down the drain, down the pipes that connected with other pipes, further and further away from her body standing in front of the sink, miles away perhaps, in another body of water, in another time, a new life for red fluids that loathe mystery and were not ashamed of it, *not unlike the process of becoming,* she thought, as the water's color faded from red to rose to clear and as she noted the wrinkles forming on her fingertips, the patterns of skin that revealed to her the passage of time and the excess of her own existence, she let out a slow, uneven breath that barely masked the start of a slow, uneven sob, and even the inexhaustibility of the gods couldn't bring back the blood now.

She could still hear the voices emerging from her insides and in this moment she only knew to focus on the washing of her hands because any reminder outside this gesture would bring her back to reality and being brought back to a more corporeal moment that could be signified by a time on a clock or a date on a calendar would mean the return of a perpetual dash, the pain of a pedestrian yet penetrative idea, the pain of a thousand deaths, the pain that wouldn't subside even with prayer, and the immense guilt that she couldn't wash away even with the muttering and the chanting and the boiling of hot water on the stove, sage burning on the kitchen counter and the kind of tiredness that was conceivable only to one who has been, more than once, soaked through in that awkward yet familiar pose on the unscrubbed bathroom tile in their own blood and vomit. She remembered, as a little girl, being taught to wash her hands before and after any significant act, *as an act of humility,* they would tell her, *to cleanse our sins,* they would say, *to be more worthy to receive,* they would offer, and she remembered once after they had all done something terrible, all of them together, the lot of them, filthy and crude and kneeling by the river, scrubbing their hands and wrists and arms as if they were covered in radiation or blood but the blood that washed downstream was their own, the excessive scrubbing, the determined looks in their faces, as if they only scrubbed hard enough, as if they could shed enough of this skin, they could perhaps deserve to pick themselves up and continue their excursion through life, and mostly she remembered how it had felt like an eternity, and the longer they knelt there the dirtier they had felt, the desire for a complete purge overcoming them as more and more blood poured out of their wounds and though she had been terrified and though she had wanted to run away from this life of arbitration (she should have, but she didn't), she mimicked their actions, bled, all with the face of a stoic, with the face of a believer, with the face of someone who deserved the grace of God, and she knelt there with the others until she had felt ready to receive.

The hot water was impregnable. The breeze through the window contained an almost imperceptible trace of relief.

Yesterday, her neighbor, the photographer, had pointed out to her the textures on the brick wall outside their building. She had nodded in politeness, wanting to return inside to boil water and make tea (she found the ritual of steeping the herbs and leaves calming, and she was trying to use it as an entry-point into building the rest of her day) but he had insisted on having her follow him to a certain corner of the building on the other side of the alleyway, from which she could clearly remember the stench of rotting garbage and urine, and where he had asked her to run her fingers along the gritty, split-open concrete where perhaps an earthquake or overzealous tree root had overturned the street and concretized a holy, sinister, and ungeometrical meeting of upward street with wall. It was evidence of some kind of higher, incomprehensible force and perhaps on a different day she could have focused a little bit harder and youngly discharged some feeling of majesty or other capacity for wonderment, but on this day she had been very worried.

One might think to bring sacrifices to this corner, he had said.

She nodded, politely. Whirls of eternity taking shape, making course.

One might try to capture this texture, this violence, this wound of the city in a photograph.

She nodded again, head turning in the other direction to try and signal it was time to go and that he was keeping her from something terribly important, but really the squeamishness that grew in her gut like some sort of alien parasite child was symptomatic of having been away from the comfort of her mundane routine for too long, all the dead stars of the universe falling infinitely and precariously slow, and she had wanted to exclaim something, an expletive perhaps, a plea to just let her alone, and at the point before she might have done something that she might regret, not so unlike the moment after one has endured a particularly bothersome pimple on their face in a particularly undesirable location and the moment before one contemplates bursting the red pustule, allowing the bacteria to spill out and infect other nearby pores or infect the pimple even further with her own dirty fingertips, causing permanent scarring, before that moment, the photographer had spoken again —

One might try to capture such a moment, but in this case even a photograph wouldn't suffice. Don't you agree? How would you capture its texture, its essence? You can feel it, can't you?

Again, she nodded and ran her fingers along the jagged edge to demonstrate her understanding, an attempt to feel whatever it was that he wanted her to feel but more so, an endeavor to placate his supplication for profundity. She felt uncomfortable with this line of interrogation, and tried to feel instead, the texture of the browning moss growing on the hard surface, focused on the patterns of tiny leaves, wondered if the tiny creatures that once lived inside that tiny world had since abandoned their home after it had stopped raining months ago, after they could feel the drying up of their environment. *What was he implying*, she wondered, did he know that she was a writer, and even if so, why would he make such dastardly assumptions about what she could or couldn't capture, why had he brought her there? He had looked at her and had seen that her head was turned away, but what she was imagining was the story of the little girl who had a crack on her bedroom wall that would slowly get larger and larger, eerie light emanating through the crack from some other dimension, and because no one else had been able to see it, she had quietly kept her mouth shut, the crack widening and widening until it wasn't just light that emanated from the narrow opening but screams of agony, strange whirling sounds like eternity being shredded apart, the fabric of existence somehow being squeezed and stretched and then punctured at this particular tension point, appearing here in front of her and preventing her from sleep, and because the doctors saw nothing wrong with her physically, told her parents that she just needed rest, just some quiet rest; she had been relegated to witnessing this horrifying event continuously, until one evening, it wasn't light or sound or anything emanating *from* the other side, rather it started to pull light *in,* so that the bedroom became absolutely devoid of light and as she sat there in the pitch-black darkness she started to scream but the crack in the wall devoured that too and so she sat there in the utter silence, watching, as all of her belongings slowly were pulled toward the hole, the crack widening its reach, widening its mouth, widening, and as she finally shut her eyes and felt the bedsheets being ripped from her hands, she felt this story, her witnessing of it all, the recollection that there was ever such a thing, also being swallowed up by the void, but now maybe she would be able to get some rest.

She's quite beautiful, even looking away, he had thought, and suddenly he had the desire to photograph her, something about her timid apathy was bewitching, but he figured it wouldn't suit him to be so bold already. He didn't want to scare her away. Instead, he had thought, he'd go the animal route.

You know, if you ever need someone to watch your dog, or take him out, or anything, I'm almost always around.

She stared back, blankly.

Oh, I hear him barking sometimes. And during the storms last week, I could hear him. I hear that some dogs are afraid of thunder.

She continued to stare.

It's a "him" right?

Yes, she finally acknowledged. She looked down at her shoes. One of her shoelaces had torn and split apart and the shoes were both covered in mud. *I'd better get going now.* And without waiting for a response, she abruptly turned her body around and started back down the alleyway. Glimmers of aluminum cans shot up as she walked through the sheer excess of filth and funk, the sour expression on her face acting like a staff parting the Red Sea and when she heard his voice calling out behind her, she only quickened her pace and reminded herself that it was not her burden to bear the brunt of social etiquette and appeasement, this person, after all, was not someone who should or would have any power over her in a way that required her to nod so many times in a conversation and that prioritizing her own comfort was something she was allowed to do, after all, she was not so vicious as her own imagined critic would have herself believe. That had been yesterday.

Today, the city was restless. The entire continent, this entire landmass, seemed engulfed in some strange and somber ritual of sweating and shaking and racking, and the reverberations in her heart seemed to indicate the final climax of this world's final demise, the coming to a head of climactic fervor and panicked psychological collapse that, on the brink for so long now, could only combine with the trajectory of a dying sun, a collapsing civilization, or the extinction of an entire species, and though she felt that she alone could sense the suffering of the entire planet, the shaking of a world to its very core, she understood that the pain that creaked her bones and shot through her body in electrical waves was not so widespread, was not so rampantly and easily felt, and it would be easier to treat these torrid rushes as symptoms, of, say, heartburn.

The effect of what they (*they,* as in, *them,* all of them combined) had done to her was evident in the things she was capable of doing to them now, of the imagination she was able to endeavor in, of the violent possibilities open to her now. This was the effect of what they had done to her. She tried not to dwell on her past but in the quiet moments and with unwelcome heat, memories emanated like steam rising up from the black asphalt. She would return to these thoughts later.

Her hands no longer felt the heat of the water but they were starting to wrinkle. The dog looked up at her expectantly and she knew to turn off the faucet, walk over to the kitchen, pour some dry food into his bowl, and set it on the floor.

She watched him approach the line that separated the kitchen tile from the rest of the apartment. He sat and waited. She used this juncture to stare at the animal, trying to dig into his eyes in a futile moment when his posture only expected fulfillment of hunger and routine and she gave in to the realization that she was looking for something where it didn't exist. She nodded and the dog, with small but hurried strides, approached the blue metal bowl.

Upstairs, she heard the old man coughing.

Downstairs, she heard the TV blaring. She thought she could make out the sounds of a train rollicking down the tracks but wasn't sure from which direction the sounds came from.

On this floor, she sat on the edge of her bed and slowly lay back. She closed her eyes and willed herself to vanish, scrunching her eyes in an attempt to close them even more than they already were, clenching her fists, and overextending her legs straight outwards and parallel to the hardwood floor. As she lay there, her body stretched out as if floating above the bed a

few inches and possessed by some brutish and dark
demon, she felt the particles of her body squeeze
together, being pulled together by some magnetic
force, each of the individual particles coupling with
other individual particles and clamping down inwards
so that in the space of two, there would be the space of
one, this process repeating over and over again until
there was, in a brief yet eternal second, only one last
and very singular particle of dust, floating there in the
light above the writer's bed, cowardly and not daring
to venture out of the direct beam of light, one last
particle as evidence of an extended and embittering
journey into adulthood, into sleep, oh, the privilege of
restful sleep—breath having lost its role of necessity
and thought its role of recovery—and as she felt herself
disappear forever, the particle of dust assimilating into
the other specks of dust floating freely in the air in a
room hardly cleaned or dusted, and illuminated by the
light coming in through the window, like a permanent
fugitive she opened her eyes, felt all of the sensations
of a hundred wounded bodies return to her own, and,
after letting out a reluctant sigh, reemerged into the air
of the room, the sounds of the dog breathing, the old
man coughing, the rumbling train on the TV, and her
own breath steadily emerging. She has never been to
the desert before, she thought to herself as she blinked
her eyes open.

2. THE PHOTOGRAPHER

The figures oozed and fell out of the wall and though he tried to look away, he couldn't. The photographer had been walking around the city for hours now, retracing its wounds, running his hands along the scar lines and attempting to depict the shattered equations and heartbreaks of the streets and power lines and knotted trees in the only language he had access to, but every time he raised his camera and pointed it at anything — a fruit stand, a brick wall, a defendable viewpoint — he felt a bitter solitude well up inside him and eventually his eyelids would droop and his hands would join back together, as if in prayer, and he would walk solemnly and apologetically to the next landmark.

There was a visible burden on his back, that sunk-in posture like a word that likes to repeat itself until it loses its meaning, an ominous regret that continues to manifest in sores or in urges to smoke just one more cigarette, just one last and utterly glorious drag. He was trying to quit. Of course, he was always trying to quit something. He was incapable of resolving himself to finishing anything or to simply accomplishing a task. He had made lists for all sorts of things in an attempt to get organized and bring order into his life, though of course it wasn't *order* that his life was lacking (once during a job interview, he was asked about his stance on teamwork and collaboration, and for his answer had spoken about the importance of establishing

order in a group of people, the need for dominance
and hierarchy and structure, as in a dictatorship or
controlled government arrangement, had repeated
the word *order* several times like a mantra, and as he
watched their expressions mute and then shift away, he
saw the exact moment they had decided that he would
not be getting the job in the research lab yet they had
sought to fulfill the obligation of letting him speak
and finish out the interview, formality, after all, an
important part of systemized structure and gratitude),
and yet he clung to the word like a slightly-too-old
child clinging to her yellowing blanky and the comfort
of sucking her thumb in private, knowing she ought
to have grown out of the habit by now, but both idea
and action still bringing her comfort and she has yet
to find a suitable replacement for the relief of having
something soft and loyal to hold on to and having a
part of her own body tethered to her mouth in a way
that feels like she is *doing* something while knowing this
is a bit perverse, the security of a thumb inside one's
mouth, the noisy and fairly disgusting suck-suck-suck
as she lightly chews the thick skin around her thumb,
and in the predilection of wrongness and unreached
maturity, she manages to realize a complete sense of
peace. He too was stuck in his present state, thumb
stuck inside of his mouth like a child, wanting a good
deep breath and the taste of a cigarette, not because he
lacked organizational skills or patience or even a good
work ethic, though the motivation to do anything more
than slowly cry while watching trains and other slow
things on television was indeed waning, and neither
the detailed account of his grandmother's death on the
nightly news, nor the ruthless takeover of her estate on
the morning after her death was announced—neither
of which he was able to prevent—did much to push
him, either in desire or capability, into stepping into

any actual spot of light. The sunlight that was all around him seemed to separate at the seams around his body, like a heavy shadow insisting on following him around and creating a membrane around his being that reflected away the sunlight and so that even on a very hot day like today, he felt cold and embittered and as he cast his eyes at the walls and signs and faces around him, he only felt himself resenting his position in the melancholy womb of the city that had birthed him, that had raised him, and where, ultimately, he knew, he would die.

He found himself near the old diner and tried to remember when he had last eaten. He wasn't any closer to having the photographs ready for his first solo show next week, for which he had pulled a series of odd favors including making late-night deliveries of various objects and substances in brown packages to addresses jotted down hastily on notecards, but he had been wandering around all day in the heat and was realizing that he could use his hunger as an excuse to sit down for a moment and ease the strain on his muscles and perhaps wipe some of the sweat off his brow and behind his ears. Secretly too, though he wouldn't know to admit it to himself yet, he was trying to find the most efficient way to convince himself of his own ability and tactility to *work*, to *get things done*, and to *undergo the process*, put in the hours, so to speak, while also preventing himself from actually getting anything done, the fear of failure more terrifying than tardiness, and an inability to understand the priorities or consequences of certain self-inflictions on his future career.

Though one of the recent storms had knocked down the large green neon sign outside and though the darkened windows seemed to indicate an establishment

that had seen better days like so many of the other
local businesses that had given up and moved out
of the city in disconcerting attempts to escape the
radiation and economic dishevelment (the corner store
just down the street from his building had already been
occupied by a group of young and deliriously hopeful
musicians who felt like rehearsing their political
anthems late at night was a stronger statement both
in response to the *establishment* and better evidence of
their talent than rehearsing during the day when most
of the citizens were gone at work, or in the mimicked
routine of going to work — *work* had become an
increasingly malleable word, and many had gotten into
the habit of leaving their homes at the same time every
morning, only to wander the streets like vagrants, that
same stare of oblivion in their eyes as they attempted
to keep up the semblance of life and order, as they
barely held on to the scraps of life with the sort of
zealous persistence of zombies that might have been
admirable under different circumstances, but here,
had managed to create a new species of itinerants — or,
when the neighbors were more tolerant and open-
minded to the detonation of enthusiastic yet boisterous
lamentation) or at the very least, an establishment that
was not yet open for business though the watch on the
photographer's wrist indicated that it was nearly three
in the afternoon, so the photographer nudged open
the boarded-up door to enter a depressingly bright
eatery with hideously yellowing walls that seemed
to be peeling away at the edges, exposing the seams
of the drywall and because the windows didn't let in
any light and were now almost completely opaque
either from the radiation affecting the chemistry of
the glass and plastic — or, more likely, they had never
been cleaned and the layers of grease and oil and
syrup had constructed a rather thick layer of defense,

and the fluorescent lights above made up for any
lack of brightness—and as the lights flickered and
a discomforting but steady din and drone emanated
either from the lights or from the belly of Hell, the
photographer lost his footing for just a second before
he realized no one had seen the embarrassing spectacle,
quickly composed himself, and, now overcompensating
for the apparent uncertainty of sure footing, continued
walking toward the counter. The shifting lights made
him feel even more exposed, though like the sunlight,
the brightness seemed to stop where the edges of his
body began so the light skin of his hands and cheeks
constantly looked as if in shadow, and for a moment
he could forget the pain eating away at his ligaments,
that hungry emptiness that propped up his body like
a dog's chew toy, but then he saw the tailor sitting at
the stool at the end of the bar, on his lunch break no
doubt, and sent over a nod in recognition. Without
saying anything, he sat down at the opposite end, a
slight release of pressure as the weight of his body
sank down onto the weathered stool. He wasn't quite
ready for one of the tailor's monologues today and
so, after ordering his usual of two hard-boiled eggs
and a tuna sandwich, set his camera down onto the
counter and busied himself with looking busy, pulling
out a small, blue, square cloth with frayed edges on
one side and proceeded to clean the lens, though he
was well aware of the fact that he had scarcely even
removed the lens cap more than a couple times today,
and save for the residue of light dust and street grime,
the ritualistic cleaning was obviously and very much
for the sole purpose of helping him to deny to himself
that he had accomplished absolutely nothing today
and that he had hardly earned his lunch, and as the
guilt and shame welled up in the corners of his eyes he
busied his fingers with checking and double-checking

the various settings on the camera, this camera, which
had belonged to his grandmother's third husband
who had left her, like the others, and was the last
remaining evidence that his grandmother had even
existed—she had picked out the camera as a gift for
his fourteenth birthday and though he had gone on to
study photography at the local and fairly prestigious
university, he hadn't thought to pull out this camera
until just a few weeks ago, possibly a sentimental
gesture in reaction to the official news of her death—
but also possibly a completely unrelated response to
the strange series of thunderstorms, as he suddenly
recalled that the lens on this model did slightly better
in the patterns of light that he was noticing now in
the city. His birthday was next week and he would be
turning twenty-seven. The intensity with which he felt
the tailor's eyes staring at his forehead was felt in the
form of heat, an uncanny laser pointed at the space
between his eyes, and so he felt compelled to look up
and make a certain quota of eye contact to release some
of the tension that had built up inside his skull.

*On a strict deadline today, barely any time to eat. You know
how it is,* he muttered, nodding vaguely in the direction
of the tailor to add another layer of acknowledgment,
but not looking too directly into his eyes so as to
not accidentally initiate any further conversation
or mislead the other into thinking that he might be
amicable to social conduct today. He couldn't commit
to the monologue and neither could he commit to the
dialogue. His upper body seemed to be in revolt and
he felt his left eye twitch and in the periphery of his
view he saw a paper bag being pushed in his direction
and he immediately grabbed it, counted out a few bills
from his back pocket, and stumbled back out onto
the street. The comfort of concrete had him breathing

more steadily and stealthily, and he thought he might just sit for a moment on one of the benches in the park, watch the humdrum of people, these enviable common folk who were unsuspecting of this being the last day, or the second to last day, or one of many days, or a day like any other.

When he got to the park, the benches were all occupied, and so he settled for sitting under the large oak tree near the eastern entrance. He sat down with his back resting against one of the giant roots, and before he could reach into the brown paper bag, noticed a large, black ant crawling up his arm. He stared at it for a second and questioned whether he should be more respectful of life, that is, he thought about whether he ought to buy into the guilt trip that his friend, the psychic, always put him through about the sanctity of life and how he ought to be more positive with his thoughts, that the energy he put out into the world was the energy he would be receiving back, and that if he could respect the significance and role of every living creature, he could recognize the significance and role of his own life in the vastness of the universe. For a brief second he thought about how great it could be to live his life this way, to buy into the idea that a smile, as a gesture, could have such widely conducting and receiving consequences, that he could rid himself of the feeling of being overwhelmed in a world such as this and just eliminate that petulant whine at the bottom of his throat just by doing the things he was supposed to do, to not think of life as a struggle but as a gift, to not be dominated by the coldness of death but by the warmth of the sky, to be able to listen to and capture the beauty of this city in his photographs rather than be frightened by the untranslatability of what he saw in the cracks, to be able to turn the ambiguous howl that emanated from the memory of failure into a squeezing and calming whisper, *if only I could give into all that positivity*, he thought, and he tried to close his eyes and think of the ocean and the sand and the feeling of the sun on his skin, and then he thought of the depths between the shallows, of the monsters lurking in the alleyways, of death and despair, of the unmistakable stench of death that surrounded him, even now, and he felt the wind howling behind his ear, even in the heat the wind did not cease to croak and shout blasphemous intentions at anyone who would listen, and he opened his eyes again and saw the ant, still, and flicked it away with his finger.

He took a bite of his sandwich, which gave him some immediate relief but he could feel the pain between his shoulders return and he only knew to take another bite, and then another. Even before he had finished chewing or swallowing the soggy bread he took the next bite to keep his mouth full, to keep his worries inside his skull, to keep the light and the ants away.

In the distance he could see an old lady feeding the pigeons, or at least trying to feed the pigeons. She was scattering sunflower seeds at the crowds but the pigeons seemed to be preoccupied with something else.

The ground beneath was damp, and though on another day he might have gotten up to find another spot, he was in the mood to follow through with commitment, to find satisfaction in the dissatisfaction of life, and was motivated today to move toward the end of his life and die (*dying* after all, a synonym for *living*), not out of weakness, but out of fulfillment, and that perhaps even in the obtuseness of his habits, he could find a formation of ritual and gratitude that might finally lead him out of this city where he might believe again, sincerely and wholeheartedly, in the power of order, and instead of the deficiency with which he believed he now lived his life, never quite living up to anyone's expectations, or at least the expectations he believed were being set up for him, he might extinguish some tiny bit of anguish by continuing to suffer through the damp ground, now soaking through his pants and starting to soften his skin, ballooning the sensitivity of that epidermal separator between his body and the earth and realizing now that the consequence of his decision would be to walk home with the chaffing of wet pants beneath his inner thighs, but even that, he thought, might not be so bad.

He finished his sandwich and looking down at the crumbs on his lap, thought, this mistake wasn't worse than any other mistake he had already made, that at least this wasn't a turning point, and yet, he realized too, that turning points were often made up of many tiny events and gestures that began to piece together like a pattern of spells that, devouring the conviction of the spellcaster, begin to inspect the actions surrounding the hands of the willing party, and instead of retreating into the fog or into the deep recesses beneath the ground where magic often stays and dwells, would rise to influence further actions and gestures, and he raised his head and looked up as if posing for a photo but knew very well that he was not nor ever would be, stationed on *that* side of the camera.

3. THE BIRDS

Look at the word *columbarium,* which means something
like *an area in a garden or church where urns are held.*
Literally, though, *pigeon house.* If one goes there looking
for pigeons, one doesn't find pigeons—first, because
the gate is always locked, especially in light of the
numerous recent vandalisms; second, because the
pigeons turn out to be doves, much closer to greatness
and metaphor than pigeons; third, because the pigeon
makes a home anywhere and doesn't want a house
in a garden, or at least a garden that is considered to
be such and called a *garden* rather than the miserable
and ragged roofs that they are more accustomed to.
If someone asked you what was the most impressive
animal event you've seen, you might give one of the
following answers: that you once watched a pigeon
grooming itself in a lit green traffic light and when
the light turned from green to red, you lost the bird
in shadow, dioramic; that you once saw a deer that
an eagle had placed on a power line except you didn't
see this yourself, only heard about it from a slightly
less than reliable source and you had so much trouble
picturing the escapade that you had to research the
weight an eagle might be able to hold while flying; that
you once came across two snakes writhing in agony or
pleasure on the path in front of you and you weren't
sure whether to be frightened by the sight or aroused
and then when you felt a stir between your legs quickly

turned your thoughts into fears; that you once saw a full-grown bear steal a pie off a window ledge except you didn't really see this yourself, only read it in a book or glimpsed it in a movie perhaps.

Even after they tore off the soffit and yanked out the planks from under the church roof, even after they bulldozed through the nave, the pigeons didn't leave. There hadn't been any reason to take the church apart. The church had been a fixture, though forlorn and unaware, it had stood for countless years, even after the fire almost a decade ago, which hadn't taken any lives but had contributed to the loss of faith after a desert saint had appeared in a dream of one of the parishioners and had warned of the corruption of the church, the fire being the final evidence of the saying, *karma's a bitch.*

The pigeons had claimed it as their sanctuary, but perhaps something about safety codes, or the density of pigeons, or a stalled development contract had prompted the sloppy and cruel demolition project. The pigeons didn't leave after all that, even though there wasn't any room for them. Their nests had been destroyed, and there was barely enough room for them to huddle side by side, the pigeons trying to hold each other awkwardly in the rain, wings flapping and clumsy without arms, trying to stick together in the grueling heat, the warmth of the sun coupled with the warmth of the reflecting concrete. People started to notice though, that the pigeons seemed to have lost their will to live. *Were they depressed?* They wondered. *Did pigeons get depressed?* It seemed logical that they could easily uproot and move, simply fly away and find a new place to roost in the vastness of this gradually emptying city. Some of the citizens of the city felt sorry for the pigeons, brought them sunflower seeds,

tried to lure them into the park where there were
lots of prime trees for roosting, even tried to bring
them home with them to keep as pets, but instead,
the pigeons wandered out into the middle of busy
streets and waited for oncoming cars to hit them. They
wanted to get hit, and they learned how to get hit more
efficiently. If they stumbled out onto the road too early,
the cars would swerve out of the way, the preservation
of life an instinctual reflex in the drivers, so the pigeons
learned to wobble out onto the road when the cars
were already a few hundred feet away, and in that
flash of time in which they waited for death, they knew
not to expect redemption or light and instead forgave
themselves, and they knew not to expect anything on
the other side and so instead savored the taste of the
last sunflower seed they had digested from earlier in
the day, beak slightly ajar, ready conditional, final.
Too, there were those pigeons that didn't await death
in oncoming traffic and simply starved to death,
refusing to leave the church or to even fly the short
distance down to the sidewalk where mountains of
sunflower seeds had piled up in homage to the pigeons.
When their bodies had given out, they dropped to the
ground, the bodies of dead pigeons piling up next to
the piles of sunflower seeds.

Generations of blasphemous beings, sinful creatures
that allow pigeons to fall from the sky. One man
wondered: *What is to come next?*

That same man who lived very close to the pigeons,
and who used to find comfort in the warbling cooing of
the pigeons, the constant and sweeping cooing of the
pigeons that reverberated subtly and predictably that
allowed him to linger more comfortably in the petrified
stillness of morning, to inspect the eternity of silence, to
be unbothered by the color of the sky while having his

tea on the balcony, mourned the loss of that comforting sound that had bolstered his environment for so long, and without knowing the trajectory or intention of the pigeons themselves, wandered out into the street one night when the fog was particularly dense and the sky particularly low, and allowed himself to be hit by a truck manned by a particularly inattentive driver. He did not die instantly, though the impact was loud and decisive, and he did not die the next morning when one newspaper reported the incident (perhaps due to lack of funds or newly composed laziness as journalism was no longer a profession but a hobby and newspapers were hardly read but rather used to swat flies or roaches) without even first calling the hospital to inquire on the status of the victim and printed the headline, "Pigeon-loving man joins the birds in death after fatal traffic collision." The following week he was still not dead, but was sleeping rather peacefully, and when the doctors decided he was in a coma with no easy way to predict whether he would wake up, moved him to the terminal ward in the basement and sent out a very sloppy notice to the same local newspaper inquiring whether the man had any living family members or friends who might come to his aid. The notice was printed the same morning as a fire at an elementary school, though regardless, the man had no family, and even the neighbors couldn't recall his name.

On his way to school, a little boy saw a strange sight: forty-seven pigeons falling from the sky. He walked over to one of the mutilated pigeons on the ground and thought that it seemed to be glowing green, unnaturally so, almost neon or fluorescent but too he was colorblind and most of all the color reminded him of the color on his jeans when he tripped and fell in the grass and the juices of the crushed blades bled onto his pants. He wasn't as disturbed by the sight as he probably should have been, and thought instead that maybe this could be something interesting for show-and-tell at school that morning, and that this was definitely a better crowd-pleaser than the old photograph of his grandfather, a general and also generally considered hero of a great war, that his mother had found in the attic for him. He picked up one of the intact bodies and stuffed it into his backpack, then, noticing the time, sprinted off in the direction of school.

4. THE WRITER

When she was just a little girl, her mother was killed
by a strange object that had fallen from the sky. Her
mother had been on her way to pick her up from
school, and only a block away, a large metal object
zoomed down with a sharp and angled whoosh sound,
striking the exact center of her mother's skull. She had
been waiting outside on the school steps, and because
she knew her mother was quite busy and often late,
assumed that her mother had been delayed at work,
perhaps with another angry client unhappy with
their haircut and demanding a refund, embarrassed
probably because when they looked into the mirror
it was the same ugly face staring back at them and
they had foolishly thought that a new haircut might
improve the appeal of their face, add the probability
of the use of an adjective like *handsome* or *refined*, and
instead of making peace with the fact of their own and
natural ugliness, blamed the hairdresser for a sloppy
job, screamed something about incompetence and lack
of *respect*, utter respect for the customer, and ensured
a dramatic and memorable scene before exiting the
establishment. In these cases, it was important for the
client to let everyone else know who was at fault for
their ugliness, that of course ugliness was endowed by
people like hairdressers or tailors or shoe salesmen,
and that it wasn't biological or natural in any way,
because that would be like admitting, too, that they

were also quite ugly on the inside, legitimate evidence of an unconscientious and brutish soul, and something that could never be reconciled because the devastation of accepting such a fact would inevitably cause a stroke or wrinkles in an unwilling patient such as this, the kind of people, that is, who already invested too much stock in the *look* of things and didn't think that the path to improvement might lie somewhere else entirely.

On that afternoon, the street had been empty. Not even any birds could be seen from her particular vantage point, sitting there on the steps, and like a dutiful daughter she had pulled out her homework to make the best use of her time and had finished first the math worksheet (this week they were working on the 7-times table and if she passed the test tomorrow morning she would earn the next colored ice cream scoop on her sundae; the teacher had assigned each times table a flavor of ice cream, and with each advancement the students earned another scoop on their sundaes, their progress symbolized by pieces of colored construction paper displayed on the wall, each student's successes, each student's failures, and it was the fear of being *seen* as a failure that motivated her most of all to succeed), and then began her handwriting exercise (she was to write a five-sentence story about losing a tooth and what she remembered was how when she had gone to her mother, unsettled with her ability to jiggle her front tooth with her tongue and the fear of accidentally swallowing it while she slept, her mother had calmly sat her down on the bathroom counter, tied dental floss around the loose tooth, then grabbed the other end, and at that moment the girl had opened her eyes, clenched tight and quivering, and had seen the look in her own mother's eyes, that slight feeling of uncertainty and so the girl had screamed, *Wait!* and she had begun to cry, afraid of what she didn't know and her mother had told her not to worry, that it would be quick and painless and would be over in less than a second, and when the girl had not stopped crying, her mother had already tied the other end of the string to the doorknob on the open door, *Don't move. Keep your mouth open and don't move,* and she had done as her mother had instructed, and when her mother slammed the door shut and she heard a *pop* emanating from her mouth, had run her tongue over the empty space in her mouth, unsettled by the gap, and then tasting blood, had begun to cry again).

When two hours went by, now on the unreasonable side of what could be considered a reasonable delay, and the moon, as yet incomplete was beginning to rise, she decided she ought to go look for her mother and headed in the direction of the shop where her mother worked. Just a block away, she found the body of a woman lying on the sidewalk, a woman she recognized as her mother from the overdetermined bun of dark hair and perfectly straight bangs (the same bangs she had managed to inherit, or was forced to inherit, as when your mother is a hairdresser you give in to the aesthetic whims of the adult holding the scissors), arms sprawled beneath her at unnatural angles, her legs bent and one of her kneecaps protruding outwards, and her head pierced by something silver and gleaning, blood still oozing out of the point of entry, the object almost vertical and erect like an expensively commissioned modern sculpture outside of a public or financial building. Near her mother's body she also noticed a dead pigeon, but she could only grieve one body at a time, and with the shock of arriving to such a scene, she wouldn't be able to properly grieve anything else for many months, though the bodies of dead pigeons

and other animals would continue to arrive around
her and in her presence, the bodies would transform,
not into bodies to be mourned or buried, but corpses
interwoven into a landscape of death and fortitude and
fear and hardness, and it was the hardness most of all
that would overtake her capacity to *feel* and though she
felt everything, would deny the sensations of *feeling* for
a very long time.

The doctors told her that her mother had died upon
the object's immediate impact, that she hadn't suffered.
She wasn't sure how this was supposed to console
her. *Dead was dead*, she thought. Her mother had been
a beautiful woman and at the moment of notification
she was more disappointed that her mother couldn't
be displayed in an open casket than the fact that
her mother was dead. *What did dead mean anyway,*
she thought, her beliefs on death exaggerated to the
extremes of grimness and annihilation. She was only
nine years old at the time, and hadn't yet learned what
life might be like for a girl without a mother, hadn't
yet learned what role a mother might have to play
in the upbringing of a girl in such a world, hadn't
yet learned that the world was large and to be alone
in the face of unknown treason could push one to
endure unspeakable things, to do unspeakable things,
to become unspeakable things, to constantly *become*
in the process of retaking and reclaiming, hadn't yet
learned that death meant *gone* but not *gone* in forever
and utterly wiped from existence, which is what she
thought and which would have been easier, but *gone*
in terms of all physicality and tangible evidence, yet
the ghostly memories that haunt and taunt and tease
and affect the core of one's actions in such a way to
push one to the brink of a binary existence, like the
trope of a kind of detached object that becomes a

ghost, possessed and unpossessed and the attempt
at a dignified life without history, these memories
would tear at the veins around her heart and though
seemingly unjustified to any other conscious being
outside the particular sensating body that could feel
this simultaneous absence / presence, to everyone
else, the diagnostic reply would simply repeat itself:
You should be over it by now. Move on and live your life.
And though that was precisely what she was doing,
with the hardness welded into her cheeks and eyes
and her mouth restricted from edging upwards even
in the slightest, she could feel the tether of that first
significant event and all of the other significant events
that would unfold because of the initial death.

They took her in and she was grateful at the time — she
didn't have anywhere else to go, her mother had left
her own family behind in a land faraway to be here and
she didn't know anyone's names, and she had never
known her father though her mother had mentioned
him a couple of times: *Your father was just another cruel
white man, we don't need him, I know he gave me you, and
that is the most precious gift I've received, but each gift has
its limits, and we don't go begging back on the other side, we
will never go back there,* and another time, *Men are all
wolves. All of them. Don't ever trust a man. All he wants is
your body, to own you, to possess you. Don't think any of them
are different. You are stronger than they are. That's what
your father was afraid of, that I was stronger than he was.
And that is why he left us, he wanted to own us, and couldn't
settle for less* — but as the sun set behind her and as she
entered the unfamiliar apartment, she knew to fear the
sky and though she could appreciate the integrity of a
scene in which the convergence of human beings here
amounted to some gesture of compassion, perhaps,
all she could think about was the possibility of the

transposition of one for another, about what might be implied in the tremendous amount of faith required to recognize that sometimes a death means something when a life means nothing, that to the last breath and moment of the violation called living, the persistence of heartbeats is neither noble nor definitive, that this wasn't implied by *lived*—this wasn't *lived* but *died*—that perhaps in death one would receive something they never had in life. She was not afraid, therefore, of what she might have to face, naively and purposefully she maintained the kind of optimism a girl can only have at that age, having been shielded by a mother who had already encountered and endured countless tribulations, and so as she crossed the threshold into a new house, a new life, she could still hear the tender and faltering voice of her mother, the subtle and solemn kiss goodbye on her forehead that morning before she had left for school, that kiss undistinguished in every other way except that she had been there, with her mother, together, and in an instance, to the last, it was this magnetism between two bodies, this feeling at a distance between a mother and daughter, between her and the hearts of every single human being either of them had felt anything for in every moment of their lives, this was the departure that occurred, that she stepped toward, borrowed, an intersection of intents and proposed fidelities, the purposeful and respectful thrust toward the end that marks, not a separation of life and death, not even the finality of life marked by a sharp metallic object falling from the sky, but the thrust toward the most articulate and merciful tribute to other human beings, the belief in life, the belief in continuity, the fidelity of feelings and to gestures and to boldness and to the worthwhileness of it all, even with that tinge of naiveté, even though she had already stopped believing in all of it, she attempted to find that historical form, if only of the unconscious predilection of amenity, for, the pomposity of such a word: *survival.*

She held onto a line from a book she had read recently with her mother: *It's a far, far better thing I do than I have ever done; it is a far, far better rest that I go to than I have ever known.* She tried to emanate what might be construed as a sigh of relief.

On the first morning in her new home, she thought she was waking up to the smell of fried eggs and bacon. She awoke excitedly, thought perhaps this really could be a new beginning for her, that she might perhaps learn to claim a kind of normativity that had always seemed out of reach, to learn to honor the memory of her mother as a guiding light, a cherished ghost, to learn to hone the unsettled unsettlingness of separation, to gain strength from ruin, to grow into a human being who could be admired and respected for their baroque fidelity to persistence, not unlike the stories of powerful women she had heard from her teacher, inspirational and uplifting journeys of hardship and perseverance, but she had not yet learned that those stories had all originated from a world very different from the one she now lived in, that *perseverance* could easily become sentimentalized into strength, though the rim that marked the edge between exclusion and domesticity was deteriorating into itself, and that the smell she had woken to was not the smell of breakfast cooking in the kitchen but the smell of thousands of trees burning from a wildfire that had already consumed four thousand acres during the night (was it the trees she had heard screaming during the night, or cats?), and later that day she would receive the news that an entire encampment of people in the woods had been destroyed—they had been asleep and hadn't heard the sirens (if they had sounded the sirens at all) —and with that fire, what remained of any fidelity to a family line, any fragile yet binding obligation of blood or loyalty to a tribe, had also turned into ash along with the unpretentious and devilish seduction of *the good life*, and as she looked out the window to see the hills on fire, the sky still ablaze and reddish, the clouds the color of dried blood waiting to be picked off piece by piece, and outside her room, the creaking of the old pipes, she realized, in fact, she was very much alone.

5. THE OLD MAN

The old man, with the mentality of an archivist, likes
to constantly organize and reorganize the objects in his
apartment, not to maintain a sense of order—he has
given up on any hope of exerting any real control over
any situation, including his own—but in an effort to
constantly refine various and more efficient methods of
archiving, of organizing information, of categorizing, of
understanding, of studying, of existing, and therefore,
of becoming.

His morning routine consists of first, hefting his body
out of bed, his bones are rickety now and his back
often misaligns itself during the night, so there is
some harumphing and wriggling to position his body
upright, and though this description sounds like one
of a beached whale struggling in the sand, patches
of drying seaweed strewn about around his body,
the scene probably more resembles a child who has
fallen down the stairs and is flailing his arms to try
and grab onto the railing again in an effort to right
himself. It is a slow process, but once he feels at a
sufficient angle to shift the weight of his body onto
his feet, he lifts himself up and proceeds outside to
his small balcony where he can see the city laid out
in fields, the positions of the buildings and the people
now appear like tiny different colored dots at the
ends of various branches, branches of other branches,

branches and subbranches unfolding into a vast and hierarchical system of classification; he observes the patterns of the people moving below with an obliquitous scrutiny, the patterns of movement both the same and different every day, and with a gusto that even Carolus Linnaeus could have appreciated, he groups the moving organisms into their varying categories, the categories changing each day to match the micro-resistances and adaptations that organisms inevitably undergo, and this, he thinks, is the key to understanding the logic of the world, the intertwined systems of disguised chaos he knows only need to be investigated further, perlustrated, penetrated, and that everything could be explained as a system, as a subset of another system, in relation to other systems, and he only need keep looking.

This morning he counts 17 people walking east and only 12 walking west, towards the park. Of those walking east, 11 seem to be in a hurry. He notices the bodies of at least 7 dead pigeons on the sidewalk outside the building, but only 2 of them weren't there yesterday, and there may be more, but his vision isn't what it used to be and as the bodies no longer get cleaned up or removed, the avian corpses live out their entire cycle of decomposition out on the hot, black concrete, steam seeming to emanate upward from their still-warm bodies, stench curls reaching out toward willfully ignorant passersby like pea tendrils that can be trained by the wind's touch though immune to spiders seeking more scaffolding for their constant web construction projects. He thinks he sees at least two faces in pain, though it is hard to describe a pained expression, and it is, perhaps, more of a feeling in the gut, that feeling of unresolved resentment from the overwhelming odds one individual finds himself standing against, that constantly emerging feeling that emanates from the bowels, a certain formation of muscles that translates into an elongated thread built upon empathy and injustice and he, now an old man who has had his own share of betrayal and despair, can understand the fugitive nature of the signals in their eyes, eyes shifting from left to right at a certain accelerated pace, at a certain urgent urging. He often sees people entering the alleyway on the far side of the building but the angle of his balcony doesn't afford him a view of inside the alleyway, just the edge and only if he leans out over the railing, an action he takes sparingly as the last time he leaned out to allow his gaze to follow a hooded man enter the narrow passageway, he dropped his glasses onto the neighbor's balcony below and he has not yet had the provocation to make the trek downstairs to retrieve them.

After he feels his lungs both full and idle from the outside air, he prefers to concentrate on the self-prescribed task for the day after he has had his coffee. The process of making the coffee is slightly different each morning as the retrieval of the coffee beans (sometimes pre-ground, and sometimes whole beans) depends on the previous day's organizational structure. Yesterday he had the coffee pre-measured in Ziploc bags and sorted in the freezer according to vertical position inside the coffee can (that is, the ground coffee scooped from the top of the can is located closer to the front of the freezer in an effort to mimic the organization that gravity would lend to the consumption of coffee stored vertically in a metal can), and as he pulls out a bag and prepares the hot water, decides he will employ a different method for the coffee next; after watching a documentary on the impact of plastic on the ocean, environment, and human health, he has resolved to decrease his reliance on plastic receptacles.

His spices are all currently organized in alphabetical order on the bookshelf like a spice shop display. The books are currently stacked in piles under his bed according to paper thickness and weight. The suitcase that previously occupied the space under his bed is currently holding his collection of expired prescription eyeglasses organized chronologically and with tags that indicate the now outdated prescriptions of the lenses.

He has given himself the tasks today of reorganizing the spices by country of origin, to offer a different perspective while cooking and preparing food and to perhaps force himself to appreciate the mileage of these tiny quantities of powder and dried plant matter, but too he does not know the provenance of all of the spices he owns and this will require quite a bit of research and perhaps a few phone calls to trusted sources, and compensation for the historical trajectory of territorialization on a map in parallel to nationhood and national identities, and this morning he has a headache and is not ready to begin the task of mapping out the spatial and geographic dependencies and codependencies between various dried leaves and colored powders and so turns on the television to see what is playing. This is a tactic for distraction, though the "work," too, is a tactic for distraction from something else entirely.

The other night he was riveted by a program in which he was able to witness the entire journey of a train that traveled from East Corkin to the Tower Desert. The entire program lasted eleven hours, the same length of the train ride itself. He would hear the sounds of the train emanating from multiple directions, not just

from his own television, and he could swear the entire
building was tuned into the program, or, perhaps, he
had simply felt *that* present in the whole experience, a
strange sort of throwback to a long train ride from his
youth, his legs dangling over the institutional blue seat,
his eyes glued to the smeared and dirty window—his
mother sat beside him in a cream-colored dress and
most of all he remembered her smiling over at him
as he took in the view, the rolling hills, the quickly
changing landscapes, all of the ecosystems that were
so different from his own, and he remembered too that
she had saved up for months to provide him this luxury
as he had begged for a glimpse, just once, perhaps
for his birthday, and she had agreed, of course, she
agreed to everything and found a way to make things
happen when it was a matter that concerned him,
she felt she was remaking herself and undoing her
past mistakes perhaps through providing her son the
kind of contentment she felt he deserved, a boy with
an absent but overbearing father, and yet, she knew,
and he would come to know later as well, what she
was really making was an object of attachment and
codependency that was fostered in the familial intimacy
of a mother reaching over to hold her son's hand,
knowing what she was really placing her hand on was
a vessel, a vessel that could never be filled, a gesture
that dismissed aspiration and became a labored and
consistent one—and what he remembered most were
the trees, the various greens rushing by like whimsical,
vegetal lyrics of a long and beautiful song, one that
he didn't know the words to, and as much as he tried
to adjust his posture, to listen and feel with his entire
body, to learn to *attune* himself with the immediate
surroundings, he would only find fragments of self-
preservation in the archives of facts, lines connected
to other lines, an archipelago of desire that quickly

became translated into an intimate and reasonable sort of order, the order with which he lived according to, the order with which he had normalized his obsessive tendency for spectating, and the externalization of an intense grief he had failed to navigate internally. He hadn't been able to sleep for the duration of the journey as he hadn't wanted to miss anything in case a rare bird might fly by on screen or a fight between strangers might break out on the train. Of course not much happened, but the sense of movement was such a horrifying relief, and he had sat so still in his chair and perhaps this is why his joints ache especially today.

Today the program seems to be focused on a live feed of a group of brown bears salmon fishing in Alaska. From time to time, the camera awkwardly zooms in and out, like chest stutters, the camera perhaps being controlled remotely by an underpaid operator with periodic feedback from a supervisor in the mode of *There, move a little bit to the left. No, to the right again. Get in closer on its head.* Something about the camera movements makes this whole scene seem rehearsed, as if editing implies intention, and yet he understands that these are *wild* bears doing what they would normally be doing in the *wild*. He wants to jump into the screen, into the sound of the water rushing with the bear standing calmly and majestically in this imperturbable place, he wants to feel too how cold the water is, how he might wince initially as he dips his fingers into the stream and then allow the chill to transform into a refreshing lingering, and then, a bird lands on a log behind the bear, as if cued, as if prompted. *I am here*, it announces. The viewer can see the bear, the splashes of fish jumping, but the bear's gaze remains fixated directly in front of him. After a few moments, the bear suddenly leans in and wriggles with his clumsy weight. He is calm and slow. He is not in a rush. He will get the fish. And with the grace and skill of a large brown bear, his head emerges with his gleaning prey, and he turns around to find himself slightly off camera but the camera adjusts, pans unsteadily and choppily over to the right to give us a clearer view of the bear's muzzle chewing and taking apart the fish, reminding the old man of a dog taking apart a stuffed toy, the simultaneous gentleness and aggression, the simultaneous care and hunger behind such an action. As the fish is ripped further apart, red emerges as a primary color. The bear keeps a firm grasp on the fish with his paw as he continues to pull at the meat with his teeth, glistening. In the background, another bear in the water, the water still rushing. *I can watch this all day,* the old man thinks to himself.

6. THE WRITER

In another place, not close nor far, yet connected very
intimately nonetheless (after all, there is nothing that
connects this all together except for the element of
time, or if time is a construct like so many of us believe,
simply the state of being and irritation and seasons that
cycle through endlessly and the swoopings of pigeons
bracketed by flashing lights), she kneels before a
large oak tree, covered in browning moss and lichen,
and she waits, idly, for death perhaps, the reaching
branches like thick threads that frame and reframe the
deliberation of breath, the supposed sincerity of the
intention of living, and crawling up her legs she sees
two black specks (she has read that ants are drawn
to suicide), and though she attempts to transform
the intention of this ritual into one of apology, into
a kind of impetus to regain her forward momentum
and to translate all of this into a new book, her hands,
like the thick and gnarled branches of the tree only
seem to reach toward the hospital ward, from some
distant memory, her mother lying on a cold bed in
the other room, the nurses insisting she is too young
to see her mother's body even though she is the one
who discovered the body on the street, and the nurses
insist it is better for her to hold on to the memory of
her mother *before:* beautiful, black hair flowing, whole
and erect and standing there, the smile on her face
as she turned to look back once more before running

into the school building that morning, that it would be
better to hold onto memory rather than the image of
her mother's corpse now, on that bitterly cold bed in
the other room, discolored, disfigured, dismembered,
and she is reminded of the hole in her mother's head,
is reminded that the sky holds things that murder
and with the forecast of fair skies she revels in the
quality of silence and the attentiveness of the heat
and imagines, like an ancient samurai, that she might
give into the deliberate sincerity, not of living, but
of disemboweling oneself (she had dreamt already
many nights of the generosity of suicide, of granting
a request of this magnitude) and, equipped with
intention, she captures the profound resolve behind
tearing one's own belly open, the accompanying silence
of dissimulation, equipped with the resolve but not
the blade that can break skin, unlike chopping up a
dead fish, unlike cutting tofu, unlike dying, and then,
crosswise: the tradition of ripping your bowels open,
like this, the necessity of being satisfied that one has
fully torn open their bowels, like this, the eternity
before the final strike, before the severing that comes
as a relief (in this case, it is a relief to lose one's head),
and here, because your sword is also your soul,
dragging open your wooden and dull soul through your
bowels, the eternity of this moment, the persistence
of wood against skin, of wood against flesh and the
stubborn nature of organs unwilling to tear themselves
open, the waiting through poverty that becomes
an unbearable intensity compared to the waiting of
death, the dragging of a bamboo sword inside of your
body (even in this imagining she has been unable to
provide herself with a truly sharp object, and instead
of preventing the pain she has seen is possible, has
created a grosser and more unbearable kind of pain in
her cowardice, in her fear of swiftness and mercy), to

fully realize the dream of an honorable death, and she imagines there are listeners in the shadows, the ghost of her own mother perhaps watching and listening to this great harmonic richness of pain and difficulty and expression and as they watch, she swallows, the lump that proceeds ever so slowly down her throat, watching, her lower lip quivers, watching—no, not yet—waiting: in this slow and protracted moment, one has all the time in the world, in this delivery of a sword, this contrary rhythm dictating a spurred ritual, the slow agony of this eternal *harakiri* swallows whole the glimpse, the slow waiting of life, that is, the eternity of this moment, this organic configuration of shameless imitation brushing violently up against one's bowels, this slow, delayed symphony of death suspended, ancient and eternal and infinite, and it eclipses the waiting that is the rest of one's entire life, ended only by the most generous of gestures: death.

Of course, this is only imagined, and the manipulation of her own interdependent relationship with death is just a single fiber of the system she has woven to fulfill her basic human needs.

In a dream she often has, there is a little girl wandering the street, looking for her mother among the other piled bodies.

How many dead mothers? she thinks. *How many?*

The different modes and textures of language become more apparent in darkness, become more apparent as the moths only show themselves when it is dark yet are drawn to the light, stupid creatures that don't seem to be able to be stopped and yet it ought to matter that they are moths, that they are winged creatures, that they possess something that humans don't, including the incapacity for speech.

She still does not know why she continues to write.
Once, at a book signing, a man in the audience raised
his hand to ask a question, *What do you enjoy about
writing?* It had been such an innocuous question of
course, but also, as she stood up there awkwardly—
she was always self-conscious as to her posture and
so had to direct a large amount of energy into not
constantly pulling up her pants and correcting her
posture and cracking her neck and fidgeting with her
hands knowing that people were watching and that
these visible actions would appear stranger than her
appearing slightly uncomfortable without a podium
to hide behind, but as writers so often are categorized
as being socially awkward anyways, why not use the
image as a form of conviction and instead of aiming to
be extraordinary, just aiming to fit the frame that had
conveniently been created for her, frames also being
beautiful and rhetorical and consoling on occasions
when it is more accepted to give into one's discomfort
rather than try to correct it in an abandonment of
virtue toward, instead, characteristics like charisma
and likability—she realized the impossibility of
this question, that what he was really asking, or
assuming, was that she *did* enjoy writing and that
she was partaking in this quaint hobby because she
already enjoyed a life of being able to let the air out
of her lungs whenever she desired and that she wasn't
constantly on the verge of breaking down and giving
into the creaking of the floorboards and wedging
her own body down there beneath them to dull the
creaking in the middle of the night and that she didn't
believe in God but, instead, in the power of the word
in a way that allowed agnostics to hold the kind of
faith that Abraham held, and that she might have some

kind of insight on how to more fully enjoy one's life and to embody the beauty of the sky as she sat down each evening to write. In all those assumptions, she felt herself getting tired. She didn't want to answer the question but she was more afraid of the potential contempt that would come from giving an incorrect one, and so her eyes shifted around the room, resting briefly on a little girl in the bookstore, seated on a tiny chair made only for tiny people in the "children's corner," happily and visibly enjoying the activity of flipping rapidly through a large book, almost as big as her entire body, and she thought back to her own childhood and knowing readers love sentimentality and nostalgia, answered: *It reminds me of reading with my mother, the stories she used to read to me and create for me, and so the narratives I create now are like a way of being closer to her, creating a ghost to properly haunt me.* The man smiled and nodded and she released the air that had been building up in her lungs this entire time, felt the whoosh of capability and the expectancy that had been buried in the heart of things, the details of her own journey to this point hazy and as genuinely unreadable as the manuscript she was attempting to finish now.

She hears the sound of the dog's feet walking across the floor and her knees start to shake, wobbly, as if she has been supporting the weight of someone larger than her resting on her shoulders, her head remaining rigid and she a participant in some nonconsensual initiation. She knows all too well the feeling of constant fear, the suffocation that comes with the arrow-slits of sunlight that make visible the dust particles in the empty space of the room and the enormous last deep breath she has to take before the next last deep breath and then another. She thrashes out her arms because sometimes she finds it easier to think with her body rather than

with words and so, dips her pen into the murdering sky
and thinks on her mother, thinks on the parents she
was given to after the hospital, thinks about the room
in the old church where she was kept, sometimes in
the dark, a single black rosary as her only companion.
When did you become so damn Catholic? she remembers a
colleague joking with her when she asked him what he
thought of her newest manuscript. The book had been
about a daughter that couldn't find herself on equal
footing with the rest of the equation that included
mother, father, son, so much mythology and religious
significance tied to these titles, and yet, the daughter,
only a fictional character, attempted to investigate the
root of the word *inhabitation* and only discovered that it
was a word saved for depravity or monsters, and as in
the face of the colleague who had proceeded to laugh at
her, she exhibits herself waiting and blinks as if in the
face of an oncoming car in the middle of the night.

One decisive factor for the increased anxiety today
is that she has agreed to attend a dinner tonight. Her
editor had advised her that it would be good for her
image, to emerge from her cave a little more often and
that it would *help her work be in better dialogue with the
conditions of the world.*

She knows this manuscript is unreadable and she
doesn't know how to remedy the situation and she
also knows she agreed to attend the dinner because
she won't be meeting her deadline and she wishes to
maintain the image of complacency. One of her worst
fears is that she might be labeled as "difficult" and
like the memories she also works hard to keep buried,
her inability to connect intimately with anyone is also
something she tries not to make visible.

She can't tell if it is hot today because she doesn't know

how to interpret the sweat beads on her arms, and sometimes the boiling heat has a way of claiming her in a way she can't do with herself. Like so many others, she does not know how to escape her own skin. The feeling of a necessary and precise disjunction from the body in which one is contained, inspected, exigent. She does not know how to leave for just a few moments in order to allow her body to remain in its anxiety as just flesh without the wounds of a heart incapable of resolving themselves, that sense of utter despair that comes from a life of *Yes please. No. I don't know. Perhaps.* In an effort to open up some kind of true osmosis with the world-at-large—she wants to feel the wind inside herself, not just her skin, she wants to absorb her own tears back through her eyeballs and take one good deep breath as her / not her—she carves tiny pieces of flesh out from beneath her fingernails, that part of the tip of the finger where the skin is tender and hidden and accessible and though she screams each time she pushes the blade downward and though it is inexact and sloppy, the blade hardly small enough for precision cutting beneath a growing fingernail, for one generous hour she is the one inflicting the pain on herself, just her fingers, and she can, in fact, feel safe from the crowded caboose cars and buses, from the exigencies of walking down the street under a clear blue sky, from the sleepless nights stumbling in and out of dreams that are as much about escaping yesterday as they are about escaping tomorrow. She lies down in the bathtub, the hot water hugs her skin fully and completely, all of her crevices feel warm and penetrated and she can feel the water entering her body through the punctures beneath her fingernails at the same time she can feel the blood leaving outward from her fingertips, and in this way she can seep in and out with the world for a brief moment and relieve herself of the intensity that builds up inside a body that refuses to yield itself to the constant negotiation of the eternal street and she can color the water red and redder and muddy and the success of death can meet the failure of life in this elegant dance of red around a body submerged in water, the body controlled by an overwhelming feeling of being suspended and the water that is hot and which slowly and ever so gradually cools with the passage of moments or with the intensifying of red and awareness of self. The bathroom light flickers. She does not notice and is already somewhere else, the desert perhaps, is already in transit, is already and simply not *here*, and really, that is all she has ever hoped for.

7. THE PHOTOGRAPHER

The entire sky is shrouded in a dark and rusty cloud, the sun now glowing an unnatural and hellish orange, almost fluorescent, and every exposed surface, even the palm trees and spider webs, are covered with a sticky layer of ash. The air is thick. It is hard to breathe. It feels like the world is ending. The world has not ended yet.

The photographer does not know how to get out of bed anymore. He attempts to upright his body, throw the covers off but they are soaked in his sweat and stuck to his legs. He feels the moistness in his crotch, in his armpits, in the crooks of his arms, and the beads of sweat trickle down his forehead and over his nose as his torso rises up to try and meet the day. This morning he feels as if he is about to conclude a conversation he has been having for quite some time, and though he is quite alone and can't even recall the dream he had last night (something to do with a deer in the forest, perhaps, or perhaps the deer had visited him in a dream the night before), he feels an insipid and immediate urge to release some words through his mouth, a gesture of finality and brusqueness, and he feels engaged, as if he's been debating for hours with fervor his opinion on an important political topic and has spent hours listening to the other side's arguments, attempting to keep an open mind and yet also feeling

that this time the stakes are higher than normal and
he really ought to muster more of the passion he has
building inside to communicate the importance of this
particular topic, and though it could be any topic and
it could be any conversation, what he is feeling now,
after this imagined and theoretical dialogue, is that
in this moment, this final and conclusive moment, as
if ending a grand and brilliant speech, the audience
members at the edges of their seats in anticipation and
at their fullest attention, he must grasp the vastness
of the entire world, the beautiful and infinite globe
with all its capacities and failures, with all its collapsed
monuments and excessive tumblings, and recreate
that vastness himself in words, mere words, because
whether or not the entire world will continue to persist
depends entirely on which words he decides to recite
right now, which words he lets exit his mouth, which
words he lets be uttered in the silent space before him.
His shoulders are crippled with an overwhelming
tension and he can't even muster a proper breath. In
and out. In and out. He feels as if his bones are covered
in perspiration and the sweat is only feeding into his
normal gloom. Must he say something? Can't he just
go back to bed?

The fire keeps encroaching but the city has stopped
emptying. That is, those who are left in the city are
there to stay and the population has somehow naturally
sorted itself out into the two natural categories of those
who have fled and those who have stayed. Without
realizing the fixedness of his decision, he too has
stayed, but not out of intention or persistence, but
simply for the reason that it was easier to stay rather
than to pack up his things and think about where he
would even go, and with this assumption he thinks
he doesn't belong so squarely in any category, that

he did not really make any clear choice, thinking that
in this respect he is unique, separate somehow from
the populace for his apathy or lack of conviction, but
rather, as the abstract lines begin to create outlines
in the smoke, he does not realize how much like the
general populace he really is, how *of* them he has
become, always was, always will be, that he is not so
special in his alienation and the tortures he brings
himself arise from his own behavior, his own symbolic
but mundane relationship with the world, his own
rigid determination to be above and better and more
generous with the way he carries himself, but, as his
body wrapped in the trembles of his thick and gripping
fretfulness show, he is just another compromised body
in the mire of reveling forgetfulness. The sky will
follow. All of the songs that might push him to feel
otherwise, that might push him to remember, have all
since been abolished.

The city's inhabitants wipe the ash off their
windshields like no big deal, this has happened before,
and there is no need to accompany oneself with an
old towel or rag as the ash permeates everything
including clothes, hair, skin; the people simply use
their sleeves, the palms of their hands, knowing that
there is really no more separation from this dust that
dirties everything, filth, muck, and the dust they too
will become in their impending deaths. The thick
layer of ash and the changing sky has become routine,
customary, part of the backdrop of life here. If the city
burns down, then it burns down. They are accepting of
this fate.

He wishes someone were lying next to him right now,
the girl perhaps, but he realizes his sometimes shifty
way of behaving is not conducive to convincing others
that in fact a gentle and kind soul resides behind

this face, and no, he is not convinced of this truth either. He isn't sure why he is drawn to her, but in his watching he seems to somehow see her lips transform into the shape of *Follow me*, and what holds him back isn't obligatory courtesy but the heaviness in his shoulders and the sweat escaping his palms.

Though he resents his aloneness, resents the circumstances of his grandmother's death, he also appreciates the strange tranquility that perpetual solitude has brought him, that is, he misses her, but his tether to her that exceeded familial bonds of commemoration was also one of constant caretaking; on some days she would be more difficult than normal, yell out in pain, tell him he was worthless (though he knew this wasn't her speaking, but the manifestation of her illness, that legacy of a kind heart now transformed into crude phrases and oblong screams), and on more than one occasion she had been unable to control her own bowel movements and he had been there, out of duty or love, perhaps, but unlikely to be both, undressing her, wiping her clean and saving her from having to toss around in her own fecal matter, washing all of her clothes and the sullied sheets and towels, and then, doing it all over again the next time. He didn't question it, just accepted the noble simplicity of what he owed her, prevented the resentment from creeping in and tarnishing the easy way with which he could proceed if he didn't question too deeply what it was he had to do to survive, but now that he was alone, truly alone, he could understand what she had also taken away from him, and in his attempt to formulate the equation of why he was the man he was today and what factors she had had in the deformation of his maturity, he felt the persistent desolation of a weed growing in a vegetable garden, each weed as an individual trying to survive, in a clump competing with each other and everyone else, and for this drive, for this ambition to live, they would be selected out to be discarded, plucked out of the dirt and chucked into the trash because their decision to live was outweighed by the lives of those others, plumping tomatoes and peppers and peas, pampered daily by the gardener's hands, each morning the hands that dictated who was to be nourished, encouraged, supported, and who was to be executed, eliminated, forgotten.

When he is finally out of bed, he has not managed to utter anything yet, and yet, that heavy feeling of propositioning weighs down on him. He looks into the mirror and despises what he sees. It isn't necessarily his face or his features or any particular physical attribute of his body. He has in fact, fortunately and arbitrarily inherited his mother's handsome features (or so he is told, she left him at her mother's house one weekend and never came back): a strong, rigid, civilized nose to be envied, a fairly lean and muscular body though he never bothered to treat it well, a strong, defined jawline, wide eyes that crunch in an endearing and contagious way when he smiles. He is disturbed though by what occupies this body, the learned tendencies and ghostly intentions he can't seem to shake, no matter how hard he tries, including distorting his face into the most uncomfortable of expressions, drinking loads of alcohol, and holding a hot towel to his face, these gestures as the points of leakage where his most insufferable qualities shine through, intrusive and obvious and recognizable. He would, for example, when somehow roped into being included in an obligatory conversation that perhaps included him but most likely only in the requirement that proximity and etiquette dictate, at any opening or pause in the conversation and only after a long respite of silence, he would only find the courage to insert himself with the sole purpose of correcting the statement that the most important person there had just proclaimed in a clumsy effort to participate in the conversation and because he strangely felt compelled to speak only in order to explain how someone was wrong about something. He doesn't know why he does this. Perhaps it is a way to try and tuck away some of the power and confidence of these people into his own pockets, he can't understand why these activities of proper communication come so easily to others and all he can barely do is to keep from staring at the space between people's eyes. He realized long ago that he was making people feel bad and yet he didn't care, and yet again, he cared more than anything in the world.

It was this ambivalence that carried over into his own work, even in school he had struggled with theoretical concepts around his art; he didn't know how to articulate in language what it was that he felt while wielding the camera, the existential dilemma that materialized and that he could sense in his joints as he would lift his arms up and angle the camera, look through the lens as if examining the inner profundity of what he had just arbitrarily framed, how this feeling unsettled him but pulled him in, like an addiction, the inability to *crack the code* of composition like an unconscious pull, he constantly felt like he was drowning, being pulled under by stubborn currents, but he didn't have the energy to swim to shore nor the complacency to sink, and something about the brief glimpses of the entire world below the surface that he would glean every time his head was pulled under the water was mesmerizing, as he struggled to breathe and find air he was also able to see tiny portions of this entire other world that was hidden from him, and as he was asked about his thoughts on precision vs. presentiment, on realism vs. abstraction, he didn't know how to differentiate between the intuitive glances embedded in the most tangible of shots, the sense of foreboding that overcame his body every time he placed his finger over the shutter button, that he didn't want to be preoccupied or dictated by obedience to any one particular vantage point and he would rather feel lost and aimless in the muck of it all rather than be pinned down and potentially be wrong about any of it. He didn't understand this tendency to narrativize the visual, he was transposing what he saw and capturing it into a still moment. Wasn't that enough? Of course, he knew it wasn't, and probably he was being stubborn on his own, because he couldn't understand the particulars of the various treatises they were made to read, he took a stance against them all, a stance against stances, and again it was his shame that had transformed into agility and he knew it was a privilege to be able to exercise this false assertion just as he knew he had never asked for that privilege.

Today he decides he will try a little bit harder, aim toward accomplishing something. He will talk to the girl, he decides. *I will bring her a photograph. No, I will offer to take her photograph.* He has no intentions and yet, he also had no idea of what might be considered right or wrong. He only knows to imagine her smile, she would be smiling for him, he imagines, and he only knows to plan for one possible future at a time.

8. THE BIRDS

On one particular day, there is a bird flying south while singing a serenade. The bird does not have a partner but it sings anyway, and as he has abstained from eating for the past three days, it feels faint and weak and beautiful in a way it never imagined possible. It passes laundry hanging on a line, and though it may just be a big misunderstanding, decides that life is utterly unfair, and isn't sure what to do as in the blink of an eye and while he continues to fly south, imagines an asteroid flattening everything it sees in front of him, the laundry hanging on a line, a cauterized and flexible landscape over which he continues to fly. Fairly, he is fair. Fairly, he switches direction and flies due west and then starts to laugh (perhaps the bird does not know to laugh and perhaps birds do not laugh at all or have no laughter or mimic our laughter or have no concept of laughter or were the ones to have taught laughter to the rest of the world in the first place) and laughs more loudly, jovially and understands now that life is limited and the landscape is limited and because fragmentation is inevitable, he flies straight into a turbine.

Some of the birds seem to be huddling together and everyone watches them, and in the act of watching the huddling birds, the tiny bodies huddling close together for warmth and intimacy and for the act of touch, for just that moment one can appreciate the great vastness and strangeness of the entire world around them, stretch out one's fingertips and feel the air that slices and discloses in a wholly unfair frigid cold or warmth, listen to the silence, the silence beneath the silence, the silence beneath the silence beneath the noise beneath the wild, wild noise, feel the sidereal rhythm that guides one's body and sees, continues to see, continues to look past the birds and to assert the loss of one's entire world, and for just one moment, realize what it is to be a body without a world.

It is the humans that don't know how to be lost anymore. They tell themselves that everything will be all right, and yet they can't help but watch the birds intently and closely and religiously to see what they might be able to tell us about themselves in the way we wish to know more about ourselves but are too afraid to ask those questions, too afraid to look any further than the birds huddled together in the park at night. It's a strange thing, how closely the human will study the habits of birds, animals, their own pets, picking up after their dogs and grabbing the feces with a plastic bag, putting their faces up fairly closely to the foul-smelling brown matter and investigating the lump with a scientific eye, holding it at various angles and smooshing it around with their fingers and then nodding as if by this gesture they can proclaim, *Yes, everything is as it should be.* But of course no one looks inside their own toilet before flushing, no one bothers to clean the dust accumulating beneath their own bed, no one bothers to investigate the matter stuck under their fingernails before washing it down the drain, no one bothers to smoosh around the used coffee grounds with their fingers before throwing them in the trash, no one bothers to look *within*.

Sometimes the vagrants only know where to sleep according to the birds. The birds perched on the lamppost give hope, they have decided, the birds lined up neatly in even increments, perched so calmly and intentionally. They give hope that there is order, that they are watching, that they persist. And are content. Others try to remind themselves to feel more lost, to allow themselves to wander a bit more, but there are proper procedures and necessary routes and we all quickly go back to the habit of routine.

The birds are everything, aren't they? One woman asks her husband.

They're just birds, he responds.

We have a reason to keep on going one more day, don't we? she asks again.

There are birds, and then there is us. I don't see how that's related, he answers.

She doesn't stop watching the birds, because in some sense it is a recourse for her own lamentation, and when her heart stops still and she feels, as if a lump of earth, small and burdened, she can see the birds gather and disperse, gather and disperse, and when there is a sound, she doesn't need to ask the question, *Who has spoken?*

A single bird fluttering its tail feathers while sitting on a line above the street. The wind chimes barely pause. Rustling leaves.

There is only one pigeon sitting on the sign today where yesterday there were two.

Pigeons gathering in the trees and rooftops to watch

the cats gathering around a pile of food on the sidewalk.

A pigeon swoops down from a lamppost to land next to the foot of a man waiting at the bus stop. The man notices nothing out of the ordinary.

A large bright area in the sky, brightness and orange light protruding outward from behind the line of trees. Dogs barking. A bird flutters its wings and lands on a wire to sit still. A single dog still barking.

How do the birds know to keep such even space between them, all lined up in a row, all lined up so neatly?

One bird perched upon a lamppost. One bird perched upon a wire hanging above the lamppost.

The pigeon looks at the ground, its entire genealogy in a speck of dirt, a crumb, another crumb, a march toward the next spectrum of relief.

How do you bridge the gap between pigeons?

The birds, like ghosts, haunt every nook and cranny of the city.

The next morning, the woman tries another question and asks her husband, *What kind of bird is that?*

9. THE WRITER

The windowsill was like a crowded graveyard, littered with the bodies of hundreds of dead moths. It sickened her to look at the sight, and yet she couldn't bring herself to clean up the bodies, to sweep them up and flush them down the toilet like the others, as if that final act of disposal (not the initial act of having killed them or simply having watched them die, the elegant flying that becomes a frantic pulse that becomes a slow and irregular twitch, then, stillness) would amount to complacency in some kind of genocide. So instead she closed the curtains, tried to keep the bodies behind a barrier and then perhaps she could convince herself that the dismal sickness that filled her room was peripheral, impaired and languished and trapped behind a set of green curtains. Some things she still couldn't be honest with herself about.

She hadn't left the house in a week. She was worried about the cat. She already knew what had occurred and she was worried and couldn't help herself from constantly peering outside to see if he had returned.

About a month ago she had been drinking her tea in bed (the tea had been a ritualistic distraction from the fact that she should have been writing, and what had appeared on the page were scribbles and doodles of trees, hundreds of trees, and she had torn the pages out and tossed them on the floor, then, upset at the

mess, had tucked them neatly into the folds of her
notebook) and had heard tiny mews-mews coming
from the outside balcony. She had hesitated for several
moments, wanting to attribute the sound to just more
strays looking for trash or perhaps the neighbor's cats,
though she very well knew the neighbor had moved
away months ago leaving behind a pregnant mother
who gave birth to an entire litter of kittens just a few
days after and though she had seen the mother and
kittens roaming around the neighborhood together,
she had seen them more scarcely and infrequently
and after failing to catch a glimpse of any similarly
patterned felines for several days, had decided to
pretend she had never had any investment in the cats
in the first place, and yet, here were the mew-mews
she had been waiting for, and yet still, something kept
her in bed for a few more moments, drinking her tea,
breathing long and deeply, gasping practically for
half a breath more. The morning had seemed eternal
and she had wanted to sleep for as much of the day
as she could muster but probably the dog would have
had something to say about that. His ears had already
perked up, he had heard the meowing outside too,
and he was already at the window, staring, silent and
curious, sitting there with the look resembling a subject
of causality. She had finally gone outside to meet the
sounds, two tiny kittens cautiously but bravely waiting
on the edge of the balcony, staring back at her wide-
eyed, expectant, the same curious look that the dog
held in his expression, not without fear or uncertainty,
but seemingly having no other option than to be here
on this balcony asking this particular human for help.
She couldn't believe how tiny they were, one was half
the size of the other, but she guessed they were the
same age and part of that very same litter she had lost
sight of and then wondered what had happened to

their siblings, why *these* kittens, probably the smallest
of the group, had been left here alone. Had they been
left or had they refused to follow or had they somehow
survived an event the others had not, though she knew
that survival was not about strength or persistence,
though these qualities were not hinderances, rather,
survival was about the tenacity and desire to go about
inhabiting a future, the possible imagination of water
rushing forward, of air parting around one's body, the
desire to make it through the day in order to wake up
again tomorrow, not in delight (that would constitute
a naive optimism creatures did not have time for), but
in the obstinacy and understanding of the feeling that
the breeze that came in through the window, white
lace curtains moving just slightly from the force of air,
that the feeling of the breeze against one's cheek as
she woke in the morning was *good*, and for that small
amount of goodness, one could inhabit and imagine
an entire future out of this sensation, could survive,
and could find others who held the same capacity
for continuance. She rushed inside and not having
anything appropriate for cats, opened up a can of dog
food, spooned some of the brown loaf into two small
bowls and set them outside a few feet in front of the
kittens.

Only as she had backed away slowly and went back
inside did they approach the bowls. They were still
wild animals, she believed, and wanted to give them
their space, so she allowed the window to be a barrier
between the outside and the inside and she watched
the kittens eating, this sight giving her an immense
amount of pleasure, the quiet sound of chewing, her
own breathing now coming in calmer and steadier
wisps, the dog sitting beside her, silent, withholding
his barks in an offering of some kind of clemency,

not to the cats but to his owner, who he knew needed this more than the cats did. She had gone out to buy cat food later that afternoon and had related her new situation to the clerk, *They really adopted me, you see,* she spoke proudly and with a smile and the clerk, a little confused, just nodded and offered her the receipt to which she waved away. She continued to feed the two kittens every evening for the next week. It became the highlight of each day, to come home and find them waiting for her outside, the soft mew-mews as a simultaneous salutation and a *Yes, we are here, and we are hungry,* her preparing their food and water alongside preparing the dog's food and water, and it seemed that the dog had adapted to the routine and was just glad to see his owner being so productive, as his canine facility for understanding held close the importance of ritual and saw that the mundanity of regularity was not a promenade or performance of okay-ness, or even boredom, it was instead the backbone of an alleviated lifestyle, the increasing regularity of her actions a signal to him of her health and contentedness, an accepted relationship with the world and therefore oneself, and when she could breathe, so could he.

But then one night, there had only been one kitten instead of two. The singular kitten seemed bereaved, but she wasn't sure if that was her projection, her own sudden and immense guilt—she had, sometime between the first encounter and today become *responsible* for these creatures, and had allowed their dependency on her to be a vehicle for her own fortitude, but, foolishly, that dependence had created a unavoidable vulnerability, a feeling of loss for something that was natural and uncontrollable (at least by her) and she had let that loss infiltrate her own sense of worth—overtook her, she believed that she had somehow let this living creature down, had failed him, had given into the arbitrary cycles of life and death and had not cared enough, had not done enough, had not *been* enough, and though she was still becoming something altogether different and these cats had something to do with that process of becoming, in that moment, she felt the wailing grief of a mother, imagined the limp body of her own feline child in her arms, and as she felt the heaviness about to erupt forth, upward from her bowels and up and out of her throat, she clenched her fists, grabbed the dog and held him awhile, suppressed the kind of manic grief that can intrude upon everything, and kept on. The kitten, the one who was here in attendance and had been the larger of the two, had seemed somewhat concerned and scared, but again that was probably the projection of her own suspicions and as she tried to prevent her imagination from wandering, continued to put out the food each day while her eyes, furrowed but attempting to be subtle to no one watching but herself, kept glancing around to see if the second one would approach as well, if he was just delayed, if he was just hiding and would come out later, if he was somewhere nearby and might be hungry too, here or there, just close by, because to her and in this moment, the distance intensely mattered.

Trying to sleep at night had turned into a series of *no, no, no's* as she kept imagining loud meows at night coming from outside, the pain of ghosts and the suffering of animals outside her window when she just wanted to sleep and that she had willingly or intentionally taken on this burden of the livelihood of these others and she wasn't sure if she wanted comfort and confirmation in the acceptance of a maternal role, living and gracious and warm, or, if she wanted a failure to be able to project her other doubts upon, the inevitability of the cycle of life and death as a way to confirm her own cycles of doing and undoing, existing and not existing, failing and attempting to move on but the past always in her back pocket like an amulet that shone so intensely it couldn't be gazed upon directly but needed to be worn on one's person at all times for fear of breaking some magical curse that might blink a person out of existence forever. And now, she hadn't seen the second cat in days, both of the creatures somehow blinked out of existence, or at least, hers, and she couldn't yet process the meaning of *gone*, again, so she would wait and hold out hope, would then extinguish that hope with a performed nonchalance as she understood the inevitable consequences of getting one's hopes up, would hope again believing if she didn't believe or have faith she would be sealing the cat's fate with her own apathy, would again preemptively avoid the heartbreak of another loss (where there had been two, there was now one; where there had been one, there was now no one) and enact a not-caring that pervaded everything including her appetite and writing, would secretly hope again, this process itself like mourning, like the wavering between one's decided inclination to live or die each morning, a supposition that encountered with the impossibility of here-ness was at the heart of why it was just so damn hard sometimes to simply be alive.

She hadn't yet admitted to herself how much the dinner she had agreed to attend a few nights prior had altered her ability to sync up again with her own cycle of alterity, and that she hadn't left the house not because she was feeling under the weather or because she was working studiously on her manuscript (neither were truthful trajectories), but because the thought of having to "socialize" with other human beings caused a sensation not so dissimilar to that of shutting the window on one's own fingers, the physical fragmentation of hundreds of tiny bones not so different from the fragmentation of self that was required to *pass* as a human meandering with some outwardly visible purpose among other humans.

At the dinner she had been forced into answering all sorts of invasive questions and remembered trying to look over at her editor for some assistance, who either mistook her look for a simple affirmation or acknowledgement of existence, or was unable to decipher any kind of tone in this precious moment of social alterity than one of normality and opportunity and privilege, simply smiled back and continued on in her own conversation with a publicist. In that moment, she had been truly and utterly alone. Of course it can be said that everyone has been in this state before, that feeling of being alone even while being surrounded by people, the feeling of being by yourself in a crowded room. The thing is, she knew she was alone, had known this fact since she was a little girl, tears pitching outwards and creating companions on the surfaces of dark walls that would morph from being oppressive limits on her own existence in the world, physical barriers that demarcated how much space she was allowed to take up, to the familiar boundaries that both gave permission and took away any burden of having to be larger than one's own capabilities, or to have to live up to any expectations because for her, no expectations beyond these walls existed. She could hear them, high-pitched voices laughing, cackling, the clinking of glasses, the questions like interrogations, and she could feel them fading away, as if their bodies were getting smaller and smaller though increasing in intensity and volume (like when one is half asleep and balls up their hand into a fist to feel in that imaginary space between consciousnesses the thickness of the air, like a ball that swells all the more one squeezes down, the compacting pressure that invisibly creates a growing ball, a circular orb inside a hand that then fades away as sleep comes), and she was fading away too while being anchored to that point, unable to even move her feet, unable to truly assess the situation furled out in front of her, and yet, a small part of her understood it all, was intimately familiar with it, knew and saw and became it. As a roaming set of eyes glanced over at her, she would suddenly become enlarged again, and the owner of the eyes would become larger, their presence becoming increasingly heavy and inhibitive, as if their shoulder was rudely bumping into her body on a crowded street, tossing her around like a balloon, as if she weighed nothing, as if she meant nothing, and any glare or stare in her direction would bring her back to that state, and when someone asked her a question, she found herself feeling absolutely unable to provide an adequate answer, but somehow words would formulate into legible sentences and would be released as utterances that arrived tumbling out of her mouth. She didn't know whether she was saying the right things, whether she was rambling, whether she was making any sense. Sometimes the other set of eyes would smile and nod and then look away, sometimes they would turn upward in a laugh, but always they would end the conversation there. Did they know that she wanted to be left alone? And so felt as if they were doing her a favor? Or, as she suspected, did they just see her as some sort of pariah, not worth their time, they were here after all to socialize, to network, to meet new and interesting people, and her status as "interesting" due to her history of growing up as an "orphan" having run out, and her status as "new" having expired when the first white hairs on her head began to visibly show. She was a girl (*woman*, of course, would have been more accurate but entirely improper), somehow connected to this group of people, but somehow without a proper label or category or name. She was nobody, though she knew this wasn't true. Her editor had been good at her job and so she knew all too well that she did have a label and a category and a name, another frame she could fit into—it was easier this way, wasn't it?—and so she must have only *wished* she was nobody. If she truly was nobody, she would be invisible, she could just stay away from the roaming eyes, step inside one of the blue magnolias that made up the pattern on the wallpaper, or just swim inside one of the champagne glasses and toss around inside the bubbles, or just leave altogether and go home to her dog and her bed and the safety of the walls of her own home, but she wasn't really nobody, that was the problem of course, she couldn't leave, she wasn't invisible, she was still somebody, still a face with a body that they looked at and talked to and asked questions of because she was still inextricably tied to them and this was not a bond she could so easily break.

10. THE OLD MAN

This morning the old man, speculating on how things might have turned out differently had he chosen a career as an applied physicist, visits a coffee shop down the street with a large red door and where stale bagels are served (though lately the selection has been dwindling, something about the foreclosure of one bagel company and another bakery on the outskirts of town having burned down in the middle of the night, but the old man tries not to invest too much in the news and to simply mind his own business). He has an urge to reach into the bagel display and reorganize the bagels according to hardness and then pick out the softest one for himself, but is distracted by not knowing how to answer the question of whether is he happy or sad (perhaps an all too direct question to be asked this early in the morning by a chipper teenage barista), and he wants to be given a reason to not give into death yet but this morning he had discovered that his couch was moldy and today he had given himself the task of investigating the meaning of "divine" and continuing a text he had started many years ago but at the moment he can't give the young man in front of him a straight answer and he can't remember what he is doing here with a pencil in his hand and the letters "Fnmmmm" written on a page in front of him on the counter. He points at a bagel indicating *that one*, and reluctantly makes his way back home.

On television today there is an hour long special on
watching white rice cooking inside a rice cooker,
on watching the skinny, hard, slightly yellow grains
sitting in the water slowly suck in the liquid, slowly
expand, whiten, then appear as a large, sticky mass of
glistening, moist rice. He is mesmerized by the images,
by how a process is dictated simply by time and heat
and pressure and how immediately the thoughts
forming in his head are of the foundation of a church
shaking and the frazzled and panicked pigeons and the
memory of an utterance: *I've looked there already. There's
nothing there.*

He isn't sure where his memory has been going these
days, and so when he wanders out to his balcony to
see the pigeons, he can't remember how many pigeons
yesterday, how many pigeons the day before that,
how many pigeons this morning. At this moment,
he only sees one, standing solemnly in the middle of
the road and the image of the lone pigeon stirs up an
incoherent sense of sadness inside him, a whirling
sensation that wells up from the deepest part of his
bowels and as he stares down at the pigeon, feels how
utterly tethered to the creature he is in this moment,
feels the eternal readiness toward death and the isle
of interconnectedness, which means if the creature is
ready to die then so is he, and that in the form he has
been given, this particularly human body, he knows
not to take for granted the preservation of truth that
others deify or vilify so enthusiastically, knows that
decisions are often arbitrary, and that one end isn't
always an end to achieving a different and necessary
goal, that an end can also be graceful and generous
or simply an end, and it isn't just a series of fancy
adjectives that turn a gesture into an artifact or apathy

into intention. He knows of course, the dangers of apathy as intention, that the entire notion of being apathetic was also a stern and rigid course of action in itself, and when the world of the past presented itself to him in the form of rain or a pigeon standing in the middle of the street, he knew he ought to at least pay attention.

Outside the window he saw the evening light, sky dimming. The evening, as usual, seemed endless to him, and though he had never really understood the meaning of that phrase, he felt the magnetization of the moon, which had moved slightly since yesterday and the window, like an eye desaturated by dust and glass, stood between him and the rustling leaves outside. He could not hear the rustling but felt the resonance as seen by the visibly moving leaves, side to side, swaying, dusty, still warm and very pale.

He imagined himself a pigeon and remembered the many deaths of his friends, bold public demonstrations on the streets and in the skies, so many winged creatures that would fall from the sky. They had been somewhat naive, thinking a protest could stop the perseverance of death, that the masses of birds dropping dead in the streets was something that could be controlled by humans, because of course humans always had the tendency to control what wasn't meant to be controlled in the first place.

When I was a bird, he said to himself, before pouring himself some water, hands unsteady and shaking. He paused to consider the phrase "time passed" and wondered about this inexplicable fear that had been entering into his diaphragm every evening after settling darkness. He ran his finger along the edge of his glass before lifting it to take a sip, to try and settle the unsettledness that came with the settlingness of night.

When I was a bird, he started again, imagining a single pigeon sitting on an electric wire, perhaps watching the sunset or perhaps watching the people below, or perhaps not paying attention to anything around it, simply sitting in perpetual grace and indignity.

A fight could break out below and the bird could simply sit, an inconsequential witness to an inconsequential event.

When I was a bird, I could confess my memories into the sky.

The old man had stopped going to confession years ago. The church had long since closed when the city had started to empty, so too, had the church. But also, after his mother died, it had been difficult for him to continue any of the relationships that had really revolved around her. He had never seen the point of prayer, though in these times of darkness, certain wounds would reveal themselves and he would imagine himself inside the confessional, difficulty breathing, sparrow hands shaking, unfamiliar voice on the other side offering forgiveness for things he didn't really believe he needed forgiveness for, and yet he pushed himself to believe in the ritual, if not for his mother, the tiny bit of conviction it could provide in a moment of uncertainty, a tenuous yet addictive balance to the way he had chosen to live his life, of order, of cleanliness, of light. Those moments inside that wooden box had seemed endless, strange witnessing of dancing shadows on walls and foot tapping against the side, a polished stone in one hand and a dead crow in the other. He was sitting just to sit, and when his mother would pull him out by his hand, he only knew to nod when she nodded and to cry when she cried, an exchange that magnified much of the tenacity of their relationship.

He had read a book on Scholastic philosophy and had come across the term *aevum*, a way of labeling the peculiar experience of existence by angels and saints in heaven. Not quite the eternal and divine timelessness of God, and not quite the limited temporality of humans, it was akin to that space *between* when one's hand was resting on his leg, that buzzing and angling of everything contained there though not visible or pointed to by language, not unlike the soul, which wasn't contained within the body nor did it exist without, but also in that sort of *improper eternity*, the intersection of indeterminacy with flesh, an ever-present but peculiar distance from the relationships between moving bodies that made time *felt*, that is, these evenings when the sky would sit beautiful and pale and yellow and rusty against an everchanging sky, the world seemed to deepen according to a certain time that felt endless yet gradual, imperceptible yet known by color and coldness. His nose felt frigid and this indicated to him a certain time of day that was known but not quantifiable, and yet, these evenings he would remember his mother and he could recall it had been exactly 2,721 days 13 hours and 7 minutes since his mother's heart had stopped beating, her yellowing face the only memory he could see clearly, the only one he clung to even while pushing her away as the light dimmed and deepened outside, the perception of color changing the course of events, changing all of history laid out like a desperate road untangling itself through the woods.

The memory of his mother's death of course was independent of the sun setting yet the twisting of his stomach tied these two events inextricably together, and now, during this highly irregular stroll down

memory lane, he felt a strange and uncomfortable
warmth creep up to where his heart might be, because
it wasn't his mother's death singularly that gripped
him, but her death had become the placeholder for
all of the other deaths in his life, perhaps because it
had been so easy for him to deconstruct and project
upon, the clearest lineage of grief that could be drawn
from one point to another. Any measure of time also
measured the changeableness of choice and yet the
endless evening swallowed any attempt at regret that
might emerge and all he could recall was the scene
from this morning: a recently dead crow in the middle
of the road, probably hit by an oncoming car, another
crow kept circling and landing on the ground next to
the dead one, flapping its wings, desperately trying
to protect the body and perhaps ward off traffic, but
none of the cars stopped, hardly slowly down or even
steering out of the way while the frantic crow was
forced to watch the body of his fallen comrade being
trampled by cars over and over and over again.

First the pigeons, now the crows, he thought. *When I was
a bird*, he mouthed, drawing out every syllable with
the edges of his mouth, teeth showing as if he were a
wild animal learning to speak, or at least a wild animal
being forced, under the restraints of the *scientific method*,
to mimic the words uttered by humans, a process that
sought to erase the unique language and way of being
of a particular species of *animal*, and to create a new
hierarchy that rewarded, somewhat condescendingly,
those animals who could best and most entertainingly
parody the gestures of humanity, including but not
limited to the mouthing of *hello*, the using of tools, the
capability for deception, and the recognition of oneself
in a mirror.

One scholar had written, *Aeviternity is the proper sphere*

of every created spirit, . . . [at] death, [the body's] distracting
relation to matter's time ceases to affect the soul so that it can
experience its proper aeviternity, but he knew that eternity
or time out of time did not and could not exist, his
mother's body was rotting beneath the ground, after
all, and any duration between time and eternity would
still fall victim to light and darkness and at the end
of the day, all he could do was wait and watch and
remember.

An image, then, of walking along the beach with
someone he had loved very much.

When I was a bird, he thought. *I used to be frightened,* he
thought. He wasn't frightened anymore, but neither
was the pigeon outside.

Stuck in the middest of his world, he smelled almonds
burning in the kitchen (had he placed them there
earlier?) and decided to let them burn, that the
memories of almonds were like layers of fog, intent and
regret rolled into the aroma of nuts, coupled with the
smell of burning, of deterioration, of inevitability, the
smoke slowly permeating into his room and dancing
spirals on the cold glass of the window, masking
momentarily that felt duration of endlessness, of *time*
passed, and in the thickness of the smoke (briefly he felt
the sensation of being torn apart and then reemerging,
like having a bucket of cold ice thrown over one's
already-shivering body, the unexpected happiness of
contrast), he could remember something besides his
mother, besides her death, besides the violence of loss
that shook him awake at night and left him shaking
there on top of his sheets until the light permeated his
eyelids. He could now remember when he used to be a
bird.

Outside, the pigeon standing in the middle of the

street, continued to stand. There were hardly any cars on the roads anymore as those who had reliable vehicles had mostly evacuated the city and others could no longer find sources of fuel, the petrol stations having mostly been depleted dry or abandoned after the shipments stopped arriving. There is little more that is as elegant as a pigeon, sitting, its erect posture, the silhouette of its beak against the pale orange sky, the slow and subtle rocking of its body as if controlled by a metronome, existing just to exist, standing just to stand, and yet there is little more that lacks dignity as the pigeon, utterly naive to the other world, one in which moments are organized into previously calculated units and counted by fingers and hands, one in which it is possible to be late and it is possible to be early. Of course the old man knew better. The pigeons weren't so naive as the humans would like to believe, and yet he needed to feel like a human sometimes too. Of course in the end, when all the people have perished, the pigeons and the crows and all the other birds will remain, their silhouettes still elegant against the setting-sun sky.

The bird sits because it sits in a mode in which things can be perpetual without being eternal. Breath enters through its diaphragm and the experience of falling in love is irrelevant to the bird but the sky continues to change color, continues to be present, continues to remain as *sky*, a formidable and concrete symbol that the world is still here, somehow yet wrapped around them all.

The bird sits to observe the wounds, extensions, oblivions, and swallowing-ups of the world, the everything else. It understands the patterns of the sky. It understands that the sun sets and rises each day, that it must eat to survive. It understands that in order to fly, it must use its wings.

The bird, like the man, is an artist, utterly tied to the
world around him and utterly ignored for its efforts.
In its world, loss is natural and necessary but also
expansive and felt and momentary. The bird, like the
man, is needed by no one but knows to persist anyway,
and because the sky asks gently and forcefully, and
because the darkness always comes, it will continue to
persist by any means necessary.

11. THE DREAM

In a dream there is a small, huddled crowd of people, their faces bright from the encroaching lava that is slowly crawling towards them from all sides. They are surrounded, and it is obvious to all of the individuals that there is no escape from the fiery death, so they do not ask how it is that they got here and they do not ask what they might do now to save themselves. Rather, in these final moments together, they crowd closer together, not to give themselves an extra breath or two, though naturally that also, but to actually get closer together, that in these moments before death they want to leave in the intimacy of each other, whether strangers or family or friends, they want to feel what it is to be loved and to be in the entanglements of intimacy with other bodies, the warmth of limbs, the prayers received from others, the tears of terror that transform into tears of generosity and gratitude, and they all grasp at each other, trying to feel each other's bodies, each other's hands, just, *each other*, and as the lava creeps further and further they can feel the heat from the steam, the skin on their faces starts to boil, those on the outer perimeter start to scream as their outer layers burn away and their feet simply disintegrate into the mass of lava, the intense heat (*heat* here is probably an inadequate word to describe the actual temperature of the fiery mass about to consume them in totality) for just a blink of existence reminding them of what it means to *feel* anything in life and to *feel* anything in death, both the joy and all of the pain, all of those human feelings as a giant and intense mass, before they are obliterated and relieved of their burdens forever.

12. THE WRITER

Upon hearing a scratching at the front door, she gets
up out of bed, half asleep, to answer it. She doesn't ask
who's there, because in this instant, her body seems to
know that there is an immediate need to open the door,
and so when she swings the door open and sees in front
of her a cat meowing in earnest, she feels the settling
of the predilection and prediction that there was a
significant reason to open the door, a calling perhaps,
and yet she doesn't recognize the cat, which is brown
with stripes and is almost completely covered in blood
and is insisting with the curvature and weight and
movement of its feline body on getting into the house,
and yet she knows too that she was waiting for a cat,
just not this one perhaps, and yet, perhaps it doesn't
matter *which* cat. She ought to be concerned for the
animal, ought to wonder about the source of the blood
itself and whether the cat is okay, whether it needs
help, which of the cat's faculties remain intact with
the tremendous amount of blood that seems matted to
its fur and legs and backside, but at the moment her
only concern is the existence of all the blood itself,
the color of it, the amount, the imagining of having
to clean the stains from the furniture if the cat were
to enter and contaminate her home, and with these
notions of concern she instinctively feels she should
block it from entering the house, and yet as she tries to
communicate with the cat to keep it on the other side

of the threshold, screaming, *No, no, no* and gesturing with her arms wildly, attempting to position her body and legs to create a moving wall between the cat and the currently immaculate abode, it manages to slide past her legs, leaving a thick trail of blood on the door frame and her pants, and successfully, enter the home. The cat is insistent, and doesn't stop once it is inside, scampering down the hallway, up the stairs, then another set of stairs, and then through several rooms full of furniture.

This is what happens in her dream although she hasn't fully given into the idea that this didn't actually happen in the middle of the night, in some version of an alternate reality and she should currently be dealing with the repercussions of the previous night's events but is instead lying in her bed with her eyes wide open, regretting so much about this week and failing to keep herself from attributing the outcomes of her decisions to her own stupid predilection for trouble and can't help but make a connection to what it is that she feels she deserves in life and what she unconsciously or consciously chooses for herself. What did it matter if she had gotten out of bed yesterday, or today, or tomorrow, what did it matter, she thought, if she didn't in fact finish her book and instead disappear into one of the walls or take a train out to the desert where she might find something resembling the meaning of eternity, something she had been looking for ever since as a little girl, a dark priest had narrated to her that there was a heaven and a hell, and that in one of these dark or beautiful places, her mother's soul would rest for eternity. It wasn't the idea of a hell that terrified her, she felt intimately familiar with a place like this, dark and hot and fiery and full of death, she knew this place already, but it was the concept of eternity she couldn't wrap her mind around, couldn't picture, couldn't fathom, and as she stretched out her legs, extending them as far as she could into the air as she felt the muscles grow agitated and restless, she imagined what it might feel like to sleep like a dead person, the kind of sleep only a corpse could have, and wondered if it might be a restful sleep, one that she could wake up from refreshed and ready to face the day, or if the pull of death would manifest in the form of desire and presence and she would instead awake more dead and cold than before, and still be bound somehow to the obligations of waking life, and just be thankful that the sleepless night had somehow still yielded her some moments of respite, the constant overwhelming feeling of being suspended in the air, a transitory figure or intermediary between realms, still tugging at her lungs and her feet and she couldn't hear anything but she could feel herself breathing and the gentle pulse emanating from the cartilage of her ear, and she tried to breathe in and she tried to breathe out but choked on the air and gave out a cough and the dog raised his head to see if she was all right, and seeing that his owner was still in bed, returned his head to the ground, patience being one of the capacities he relied on most regularly.

She remembered in the dream how the cat kept going, further into the labyrinthine and seemingly multidimensional framework of her home, up the stairs, up another set of stairs, down a hallway, down another hallway. The cat left a thick and bright trail of blood on everything it scampered upon, everything it touched, and though she was distressed, her obsessive tendencies for cleanliness flaring up constantly as she chased the cat through the house for what seemed like forever, she also felt intimately connected to the cat, like perhaps the cat needed something from her, and she needed to give whatever it was the cat needed. By this point she had figured out that the blood didn't seem to belong to the cat, but the volume of blood the cat had been carrying in its fur seemed endless, the blood almost pouring off its body in all directions, like enormous red sentences that perpetrated unreadable sins or like red cypress leaves falling off a tree after a particularly strong set of winds, and every time she managed to catch up to the cat, she would only get more blood on her hands and the cat would slip ahead further and further, the strangely regulated system of hallways and rooms in this house as familiar to her as the lines on her hands, that is, both intimate and ever present but also unseen and hardly ever known with open eyes.

The cat eventually stopped in the bathroom, and inside, let itself be picked up and set down in the sink. How did she know this was all to be finished so soon? How does a belief like that just arrive and even though she is only a few sentences into her manuscript (she has lied, has claimed she is farther along than she really is, has been writing and rewriting the first few sentences over and over again), how does she know that it is more important to wash the blood off of this cat, than to wash the blood off of her own hands?

Of course it is now morning, and in the bathroom, she can't help but study her hands closely and still holds on to the belief that she was visited by a bloody cat in the middle of the night and this morning she notices all of the lines on the palm of her hand, the way her fingers bend, the lines on her fingers, and recalls a story about siblings dragging the bodies of other siblings and a brother that only knew how to say goodbye over and over again but never leave, and though she does not

have a brother, she feels she understands the gist of
this gesture of *farewell* and washes her hands in the
sink, if only to return to this world, if only to remember
what it is she needs to get done today, if only to gather
the motivation to persist in the dragging on of time, if
only to face the day and attempt to be free for these
small moments as the water quickly turns from hot
to cold, and with the feeling of a plastic pen against
one's teeth, sees the first time her relationship with
cats really began: it was not the mew-mews outside her
window, nor the bloody cat of her dream, there was,
she could now recall, another bloody cat of her past
that has eluded the role of haunting her, and she had
managed to elude the role of being haunted.

She remembered not being able to sleep well for many
days, in that new house where she learned to pray and
to use a rosary, she learned first the arbitrariness of
ritual but also its necessity to the sanity of spirit, and
then the absorbed significance of it, how it allowed
certain details to come into vision, how it allowed her
to pay tribute to certain cracks in her worldview, that
is, she didn't want the death of her mother to cloud
over everything and prevent her from *maturing* into
a young woman, and from what she learned sitting
in the pews every Sunday with her new family, and
from what she learned reading the Good Book in her
room at night, invented her own ritual for exorcising
the silent trauma of her mother's death, that is, she
did not want to be weakened and made prey-like by
allowing one violent event of finality define her — she
could already see the looks in their eyes, the round
blacknesses that only saw her as a victim, *poor thing,
she will get over it though* — and the way to do this
respectfully, to not tarnish the memory of her mother
in living form, was to blame her own young and

compromised body of being possessed by the demon-like entity of a wound so deep that it melts you, it turns you into ash, and then, like the miraculous revival of a patch of moss that has been stored in a petri dish for a decade, with the addition of water is reinvigorated, reinvented, and then, resurrected.

The cat was old, its once jet-black hair now graying and matted, clumps of it had been lost and there were scabs that oozed puss when she tried to pick them off. She had procured a candle and sharp knife from the kitchen, and in preparation for the act she closed her eyes to see the not quite black, the darker black strings and lines in a tangle that darken and stretch on the almost translucent but utterly dark background, and she realized that this was space, twists and knots forming from the viney particles in the air, the darkness of dark space spinning and weaving and wrapping, and then a strangulation, beautiful but suffocating, and she wondered how she would ever return from this, how she would ever open her eyes after seeing the beginning of the universe (or the end, because the same processes that create also destroy, the same hands that make also undo) and after having seen it all in just in the shadows of her eyelids, the magical performance of it all, she didn't know how to open her eyes again, or perhaps they were already open, and, looking down at her bloodied hands, realized that all she had to do was to close them again. She felt the cat's final breath move through her like a colonizing presence, and the unsettling of her body helped her recognize the presumed sphere of influence around herself, and what she wondered most was what the cat could offer her that a person couldn't, wanting to know what it was about intimacy that could push a human to be capable of hurting someone so cruelly in a way that a cat was not, not in the same way at least, and though she knew she had taken something from the cat, she was grateful for what it had given her through its message of finality, that she was purged of the pluralized tremors and here was the normalcy finally imposed upon her flesh and she had kept her eyes closed until her stepmother had walked through the door, seen her there kneeling with the knife still in one hand, the dead cat at her knees, and even when she heard the bloodcurdling scream ring through her head and vibrate the cartilage on her ears, even when she felt the ground shake from the collapse of a heartbroken body falling to the floor, she did not open her eyes, no, not even for a second.

After that bargain, a bargain she felt she had made with the Devil himself but was a bargain well-paid for nonetheless, she did grow up and mature into a capable, young lady. She learned to live by herself and to not depend on others because she had seen that other people could never be counted on, not for very long anyway. At some point, they were all bound to disappoint and she just didn't have the emotional capacity to be disappointed anymore, or at least the patience.

One might think that the life she had led would have hardened her emotionally, and though she appeared tough and capable, the reality was that she felt too much and had not found a way to sufficiently dampen her feelings, the daily heartbreaks of life, even the cold, which she savored with a sinister smile. There had been a period of coldness, killing another living being does that to you, and yet the coldness dissipated quickly and she felt even more than she had before, all of the destroyed intimacies like blunt needles trying to pierce her skin. There were many examples of heartbreak: the dead bird she had seen on the street the day before, the many other dead birds she had seen on the street the days before that, the changing color of the sky, the last man she had loved (she couldn't remember now if he had really existed), the cats, the inability to sleep, the inability to stay awake.

Here was the thing, it had happened before, that is, she had seen the deterioration of a person, a soul, the slow and gradual fading away of the motivation to get up, to open one's eyes, and because she had been too tired, too tired of trying, too tired of the abuse sent back her way, she had stopped doing anything, she had stopped trying to stop them. This didn't stop the *feeling* though and after days of silence, passing by each other inside various architectural spaces, namely, their home, the silence had become just that, real and actual silence, and then, they were gone, just like that, as if blinked out of existence by her own stupid apathy and her own stupid sentimentality and her own stupid self, and though she knew it wasn't her fault (though in reality, she knew it was, and no amount of being a "victim" excused her from the ritual killing of her stepmother's oldest and best friend) and yet she couldn't shake the feeling she had been the lynchpin for it all, not just the disappearance of something called "family," but her mother's death, the birds, all of it, and if she had kept trying she could have bought more time for something to happen, for something to intervene, for a spark to be started, and as she remembered the bloody cat again and again, all she could think of was the phrase, *one for one*. The cat for her mother. The cat for the return of her self. The cat for her own damnation. Because in the end, salvation or damnation, they were the same thing.

13. THE DOG

I wake up and look for the trees. It is warm and bright but I feel the sadness of the wilted leaves on the ground, roots unrooted, and I try to find my bearing but I only feel the harshness of the sun. My scent trails have dissipated but the sadness bears heavier than any smell. I don't see the woods at the mountain's edge, instead the dreariness of the swamps, wet and damp and encompassing, the dreariness takes over the landscape. All of the pointed, elegant trees are missing from this vantage point and again I feel the heaviness, the sadness of it all. Who is crying? It seems to be coming from everywhere. Yet, the light remains. And yet, some of us are still here.

14. THE PHOTOGRAPHER

He didn't know how to escape, but more importantly, what it was precisely he was trying to escape from also continued to evade his focus and though the moment of enchantment with her had now faded and turned into a conviction that would obscure any and all rationality he might have left, he only knew he needed to explain his actions to no one and that the trembling in his shoulder would eventually subside and eventually he would leave his apartment again and he would be able to breathe as he always had.

He didn't understand, of course, whether he had done anything wrong. Ethics had never been an issue for him. Rather, in the constant desire to *do something* about the vast thoughts always circling around in his head—those thoughts about what a future might look like had he had a better childhood, about what his eyes would look like had he made better life decisions, what kind of home he might live in now had he chosen a different career, what kinds of things he might have learned about relationships had he decided to cohabitate with an animal—he believed that in a world such as this, there was more often hope in the inevitability of nothing than in the possibility of everything, and in the necessity to always justify both his current position in life and the amount of light given off by the lamp next to his bed with some *cause*

deeply embedded in his past, this constant justification
of event after event, memory after memory, he had
readjusted the trajectory of his life so many times to
suit the current context in which he constantly found
himself in that he would often find notes scribbled
to himself on the backs of shelves behind books,
dusty and folded carelessly, and he would no longer
recognize his handwriting or motivations for these
seemingly self-preservatory rationalizations. He didn't
know how to have compassion for himself, or his past
self, or any of the selves he had occupied in the past,
and therefore, he probably didn't know how to have
real compassion for anyone else either. The logic with
which he used to diffuse the anger and apathy that
now drowned his accidental actions was the same logic
he used to see the patterns of his life, so incredibly
clear, so incredibly transparent, that he could see
exactly all of the causes and effects of his person and
nothing he *felt* really mattered when he could see
so clearly the constituents of his being laid out over
the span of space and time, a clear and transparent
network of intertwining webs that could be expanded
or abbreviated, this archipelago from which he could
see in all directions, alone yet present, and he, as the
seer of all the interdependencies and codependencies,
could be free to pursue something more than what had
come before, believing that the key to the future was
in escaping the tethers of the past, and though he had
never fully faced the legacy of his own history head-
on, he believed he could repossess everything that
had been lost, that he could be redeemed, and was in
fact, on his way toward some kind of redemption now.
Here he was, now. He believed he was the person that
he had become. *The past makes the present,* he would
say. He used to examine old journals and documents,
even the photographs he used to take as he wandered

around the city and its surrounding environs, when he
would take the train out into the desert to simply see
more of what the world held and to see more of what
existed and persisted outside the city's trepidation
and treachery, when he knew still to press down on
the shutter whenever he felt the sudden happiness
that would creep up suddenly and violently, or the
heaviness of regret brought on by the embrace of a
shadow, or even the betrayal of light when he would
arrive at the precipice of sight and devastation, that
threshold where mere sight would transform into
that aesthetic despair that can only come from the
recognition of something that in its miraculous beauty
deteriorates simultaneously into the sense of impending
death and doom, the kind of realization that forces one
to come to their senses, all of them, and in the shock
of remembering what it is to *live* in a world so quickly
dying, the lamentations become gladness again, the
failings become reasons to persist, and the tears are
only a small physical manifestation of the reason why
art might yet continue, but as a result of his immaculate
resistance to relinquishing control, of the countless hills
he could see now as just hills that could be described
and quantified, he had lost the will to press down on
any button and the desire to capture anything in an
image he might return to later. *The windows don't look
out on anything,* he thought to himself as he noticed the
growing piles of bodies outside and the increasingly
red-orange of the sky, tiny particles of ash already
building up on his unmoving hands.

The one photo he had taken in months had been
of her dog, and he had done it as a gesture of the
possible encounter between human lives and other
animal species. All of his gestures, though thoughtfully
planned and coordinated, seemed to be missing the

language of silence that she had insisted on, and still, he did not know what had happened to make her react the way she had, only that he needed to escape, that the recognition he felt as something stirring in his bowels, which he could only recognize as fear, and because he was not a fearsome creature, he had directed this energy at the only other speaking being in the room and had acted accordingly. He had acted accordingly.

They hadn't had a proper first date, it was his fault probably, but he had lured her out for a neighborly chat and it had all quickly escalated from there.

So you write? I admire that. The ability to say the impossible. All of reality happening at once. I wouldn't know how to fix that in language.

Language isn't fixed.

Sure. But it's just words, right. The words don't change. You have to pick the right words. That's so much pressure.

She had disagreed with almost everything he had said, but for some reason, she had continued to talk. An hour had gone by, and she had made no signs of getting up to leave, and that had energized him, had encouraged him. At some point the old man had come in to purchase a bagel, and she had looked over at him struggling to pay with a pitied look and her earnestness had caught him off guard; he had caught her look, had been about to make a joke about the old man's clumsiness, his strange gait, his snoring, but her widened eyes signaled that he shouldn't, and it was this, not her unconscious coaxing for him to be steadier about his judgments and more careful about what he allowed himself to utter out loud, but that he had been able to read her, had been able to catch himself and understand what the proper response was in this moment of social exchange, had been able to interpret her own longing, or at least had allowed him *in*, for that brief period, allowed him to penetrate that vulnerable and venerable surface, and this was something he had never been able to do with anyone else.

He hasn't been the same after she died, he had said.

Yes, she had agreed.

Then, she had asked him if she could show him something.

In exchange for the other day, she had added, meaning when he had showed her the cracked textures on the wall outside their building. He had, of course, agreed.

She had then taken him up a series of winding streets, through the east hills and as the streets narrowed and curved and steepened, they had emerged in a small clearing that overlooked the entire city, the trees long gone, their burnt stumps as reminders of whose view this really was, had belonged to, the dry grass sprawled out around them, and she had pointed out certain landmarks in the distance, had explained to him that this was a place she used to come to be alone and that this was a place she hadn't shown anyone else, *our little secret*, she had whispered, and as she spoke his eyes had remained fixated on her lips, her small mouth moving to shape words, her lips soft and pink and he hadn't been able to resist, she had brought him here for this, he believed, she wanted him to kiss her, he convinced himself, and he grabbed her feeble body and pressed his lips to hers fervently, just in case she might change her mind, just in case she might pull away, and he thought he felt her struggle just for a moment, her hand on his chest in the gesture of pushing him away, but he persisted, let her know he wanted this too, that it was okay, and her stance melted into his, she fell into it, fully and completely, and though she felt the heat permeate throughout her body, felt the excitement rush through her blood, she also couldn't suppress the strange kernel of doubt, and she knew too that she had lied, that this wasn't her secret place where she would come to be alone, that in fact a previous lover had shown her this place, and she had subsequently brought many other ex-lovers here, had in fact never come here to be alone, but always with someone else and with uncertainty, and his willful ignorance allowed him to stay intoxicated, her lips were beautiful, she was beautiful, and he would not deny the improbable, the unbelievable, that he could, in fact, be redeemed, because he was in love, and in all the ways he had perhaps acted improperly or incorrectly after that first kiss, he had acted always and completely out of love, always for her, and this, to him, was undeniable.

His legacy of exclusion was, in his way, a way of maintaining flexibility in his relationships. In one of the maps he had encountered in his grandmother's attic, the lines had appeared scribbled, scrawled across the paper in uneven and chafed strokes. The map, therefore, was not an accurate or precise depiction of any particular place, but instead an emotional resonance of a geographical locale, and he could only guess at what must have made the surveyor's hand so shaken. He realized he had been drawn to her overwhelming but well-practiced and hidden emblem of guilt, that it was this particular bone structure of culpability he had seen as balancing out his own fear of failure. He was tired of categorizing everything from a vantage point of neutrality—the corresponding details were neglected points on something that might resemble a map had he been aware of his so far-removed perspective, that where he stood was not at the center of this charted representation of space, but in that even and steady plane whose boundary consisted of all the points equidistant from that central point — and in the realization that it was the mere possibility of suicide itself that made all humans equally existentialists, he realized he could justify anything to himself if he tried hard enough, he could justify it all.

15. THE WRITER

She had recently made the mistake of letting the photographer into her life, and then, into her apartment. It hadn't ended well and it wouldn't happen again. The circumstances of how he had seduced her so easily, in retrospect, were so suspect and obvious, and though she tried to remember these things weren't her fault, she couldn't help but feel that shame bubble up in her gut, burning, boiling, and though she had thought that for a moment, she possessed him, it was him who had possessed her all along.

What is the feeling of a mausoleum, she wondered, not being inside of one, but the feeling of *being* one, of *becoming* a mausoleum, the skin of your body thickening and hardening into concrete walls (the process of producing concrete as a building material as dating back to prehistory, a method of construction that allowed people to survive and thrive in the desert, the structures having outlived its inhabitants and existing to this day, the addition of volcanic ash to create rigid structures and vaults to lock valuables in, or to keep intruders out), that is, in this insane (sanity as somehow defined as the belief in a singular body though any nonhuman living creature understands the cycles of growth and death, inside the same body, inside multiple bodies, the reciprocity of bodies in the shimmering, undulating sea, so that of course, the shuttered human idea of "identity" is indeed an insane one) and bio-precarious domain, how does the constant trauma of the body, the constant risk of harm essentially and efficiently revise the language with which we identify ourselves, the fluctuating influence of physical pain and devastation that doesn't ebb and flow like the tide under the influence of the moon's gravitational pull, not like the exertive forces between planetary bodies, but rather like the buildup of it all, the release in the form of seizures and long, rasping cries in the middle of the night after the repeated electroshock therapies given to treat just this very thing, that is, the hysterical crying that one attempts to cure with the forced convulsions of the body (not unlike an exorcism, not unlike a ritualistic killing of a cat) is the same hysterical crying that continues to emanate and echo in the hallways long after, because there is no cure for living, just as there is no cure for dying (just death itself as the ultimate illusion for finality), so that the cry, that lustrous and desolating and calamitous force that is a wailing howl exuding from your own body, that cry is also the logic of this world.

She wondered about the complicity of architectural bodies: did the mausoleum understand the complicit role it played in the resplendent presentation of death, did the church understand the complicit role it played in the resplendent presentation of death, did the streets, the cafe down the street, her home, her own bed? How had she been so conditioned in these spaces—this accumulation of agendas suddenly so suffocating—and so then, what would it feel like to have a body without fear? To feel completely safe without harm? How would her body feel then? How would she feel differently? That is, how would she *feel* (as an active verb) differently?

She had mistaken his awkward posture and subtle undertone of shame in how he slouched and carried himself for sweetness and compassion, a kind of empathy *for* and *with* other pitiable creatures. She had mistaken his performed complacency and vacant gestures of chivalry for understanding and a genuine attempt at feminism. She had mistaken his indignance and strange sort of overbearing pride in her accomplishments, his constant flattery and attention for admiration and affection. How obvious it was now, that thin line between veneration and love, the veering between two trajectories, one that easily led to possession and condescension in the guise of worship, the other that led to, well—she didn't quite know. *Love can hold it all,* she had once heard in a song, and even now she couldn't quite grasp the possibility of such a thing, perhaps she had never experienced love in the way it was meant to be manifested—she could hardly remember her mother, and when she thought about her childhood, it was the terror of the sky that overshadowed any moments of familial intimacy—and to her, it seemed such a complex interweaving between bodies wasn't a simple union at all; rather than an elegant and beautiful consolidation of two beings, love appeared to her to be a chaotic and painful unraveling of two becomings, these two stellar junctions of hate and anger and trauma and pain and confusion and betrayal and regret and shame and sadness as being torn apart at the seams in order to be stitched back together in a monstrous and illogical synthesis, fluids leaking, irregular temperatures to be regulated; indeed how could love hold it all when it could hardly keep itself upright, keep from crumbling into smithereens; was love then just another process for destruction in the name of rebirth, and if it was, how did it differ from the apocalypse itself?

When he had first asked her out to dinner, she had looked at him with all the ferocity of a cat but the docility of a dog, knowing full well that in life there was no permanence, and because she hadn't ever named the cats, had managed to find a way to move on and simply nodded, had managed to put herself in a situation once again where she had assumed she was making her own decisions but, compromised from the start, had been complacent to his whims and simply gone along with the flow. She should have known that the question, *Would you do me the honor of having dinner with me?*, was one of entitlement, there was no honor here of course, only the possibility of dishonoring, that is, the possibility of her dishonoring him because he had been entitled to her company from the start, and this wasn't anything she was giving to him, only something that could be taken away, because from his perspective, he was only capable of seeing what he was losing, not what he might gain, not what he might proclaim gratitude for.

Then, the first night he had slept over, she had first felt a strange kind of intrusion — the dog too was confused, he was used to just the two of them, and this other presence peaked his suspicions and so he remained alert until after he left the next morning. But then, as she lay there awake, she could hear him sleeping next to her, the steady breath, the heaving of his body and the rise and fall of his chest, and this was perhaps the most calming thing she had ever experienced, even the quiet snores somehow signaled that he was at peace, was sleeping soundly, was in that dominion of tranquility, and though part of her envied his ability to move between realms so easily, she felt something like care in the knowing of his blissful state, and then, lulled by his slow and even breaths, had fallen quietly and painlessly asleep.

In her dream she had stood there with him at the edge of a massive volcano. They had both been wearing some kind of heat suits with masks that covered their entire faces. He seemed to be saying something to her, his mouth moving visibly through the protective screen and his arms waving wildly, and perhaps if she had been awake and equipped with her more rational cognitive skills, she could have easily made out what he was trying to communicate, but here, at the edge of land and fire, the heat from the volcano still felt through their protective suits, she remained transfixed by the movement of lava on the surface, its snaking movements like a giant, fiery reptile that utilized the heat as a mechanism for growth, and swaying her own body to match the undulations of the lava she apperceived the viscosity of the fiery mass and understood from the volcano's whisperings that there was indeed no permanence, no permanence of ground, no permanence of art, no permanence of life, and because she agreed that this was true, stepped forward and pushed her companion into the volcano. She could not hear him scream (probably there was no time, he disintegrated and assimilated into the lava almost immediately), but found herself mouthing the words: *It will encase your bones. Everything will melt, like water. Everything will melt, like water.*

When she awoke he had already been staring at her sleeping for an indeterminate amount of time, and she had mistaken his smile for happiness, his own joy for hers, and as he spoke her name she felt the slippage of identity, the unfamiliarity of this name being spoken to her in this particular kind of slippery voice, and because she was so flustered by this visceral reaction to hearing her own name, repeated it out loud as well, like an echo, and then felt the unfamiliarity of saying one's own name out loud as for her, and many others, it had always just been "I."

Everything had quickly gone sour after that, though *sour*, the word to describe the flavor a lemon might have, that acidic taste that might cause one to pucker their lips and pinch one's eyes shut briefly, might not be the word to describe what happened, yet there was indeed a process of souring, of the building up of anger and resentment, of the bittering of relations and in the way one's own disappointment with oneself is contagious and the disappointment becomes refracted outwards, toward the other person, then reflected back, then mutated and reflected back again, so that the disappointment in a self is also the disappointment in the other *as* the self, *sour* might be the only word to describe what happened. On the same day he confessed he was falling in love with her, they had also had a brutal and impassioned argument that had ended with his hands around her neck (and a dark bruise the next morning), her screaming for him to get out with a knife in her hand, and his refusal to leave because she was a danger to him, to everyone, to herself, and he would not leave until she calmed down. She begged him to leave her alone, and he would not, and when she locked herself in the bathroom to get away from him he had broken down the door and shook her like a rag doll, insisting that he loved her, insisting that she needed to let him take care of her, and when the guilt overcame her, and when he finally convinced her that no one else would love her the way he did, she let him carry her to bed and take off her clothes, and in the rocking back and forth, in the strange and distant state she found herself in, like a boat in the cushion of the sea, she wondered what it would be like to sail away on the cue of a simple sound, like she had never been hurt, like she had never been hurt before, *we could trade places,* she thought, *like I never hurt you, like you never hurt me.*

This happened several more times before she realized the fucking maddening limitations of *love,* and when she told him to get out, she could feel this was the last time, that she had finally, in the shame of her despair, in the perceived complacency of assault, had finally found a modicum of control over the situation, and as he begged her to let him stay, then threatened to call the police, then threatened to kill himself, then threatened to kill her, she had picked up the phone and dialed 911 and that was when—though he knew that probably no one would come—his fear of failure and his own and real disgust at himself, his abhorrence for causing a scene, his refusal to be the perpetrator in any way or form propelled him to finally leave. Unlike her, he did not understand the process of *becoming,* and only understood *had become,* that is, his own traumas had bore down so hard to form the person he was today— that is, someone who understood what it felt like to be a victim, to have no hope, to always be on the side of the beaten—so that he would not and could not ever *become* a perpetrator. This was the logic of his world.

After he had left, she had sat in the shower and wanted to be left alone and to drown and just disappear but the trickle of water was hardly enough to make her feel even a little bit suffocated and she had wished the pipes would burst and she had wished the water would burn or at least scald her skin and she had wished she was sadder and could cry more tears to fill the tub and she had wished he would come back and say sorry for her mistakes, for her misgivings, for her own transgressions and indiscretions and issues and insecurities, she had wished he would take credit for her alienation and her desire to be dead in this moment and to squeeze her tight until her chest burst and then she might feel loved and then she might be able to sleep but he was already gone and she had asked him to leave and she had hated the way he had looked at her with such desire and malice and she knew that putting her faith in another had never been the solution but she didn't know how to stop making these mistakes.

16. THE BIRDS

The birds take a break after each moan. That is, after the blood has dried, they gather around the skinned corpse of a child that lies in the street, bright red hair, darkened shades beneath and around the body. The body isn't starved, and so, works as a gesture of love, or a failed attempt at it. The birds have never been alone and so don't know what alone feels like, don't know the tremendous loneliness that accompanies a death like this, don't understand the desire to be left alone and then the immediate regret of solitude, and yet, they are just birds.

God, we are still awake.

What is God anyway? the birds might ask.

A bird notices the stillness of the child's body, a stillness that might frighten the stars, if there were stillness, but one can yet imagine the movement of hooked hands, kicking feet, screaming, the writhing, the screaming, the screaming, the screaming, *Oh God.*

A bird notices the child's closed eyes, hears its voice as it whispers, *I'm going to stop crying now. I'm going to close my eyes now. I'm letting myself be alone. I'm going to close my eyes now. I'm going to keep them closed. This is how it starts, with a pair of closed eyes. I can hear the sound of my heart beating. I can still the flashes of red. I can see the dead dog. Another dead dog, another broken television, another severed limb. I can't look away from the body of the dog. I said I wouldn't cry. It's not my dog. It's not my dog. It's just another dog. Where is my dog?*

A bird thinks, *We are all gods now.*

A bird is frightened, sees a giant spider creeping past the child's body.

A bird breathes loudly, *I am tired of being God.*

A bird confesses, *I am often mistaken for God.*

A bird pecks at the child's eyeballs. This is a gesture of continued steadfastness and persistence, a refusal to give in to the trap of sanctity, and after each moan, the bird looks up to see the other bodies, piles of them, feels hungry and then continues its task. This bird does not see any other option than this one, laid out for him so easily and truthfully, to eat or be eaten, to kill or be killed, and because it does not see death as a choice but something to run from, it also doesn't understand the possibility for essence or value, for meaning or sentimentality, and after it is done here, will move on to repeat the same actions again, this repetition as being the essence of its life.

17. THE OLD MAN

It is true that a long time ago the old man had been married, that on the night of a strong and raging storm on the edge of the sea, his wife had screamed out in the middle of a night of the terrible pain in her head, the categorical and unyielding pounding from within her skull that would not subside and paralyzed by her screams that punctuated the rain outside and haunted by each eternal moan that reverberated through his bones like he was being rattled, he had been unable to do anything; she had begged him to help her and writhed in agony, her hands clamped over her head and then a hand reaching out for him, eyes clenched shut and screaming, still screaming, and he had been unable to reach out even his hand, still frozen, still immobile, like a sessile plant that reaches and reaches for the sky, the distance that will never be crossed because the plant will grow as tall as it can and still never reach the collapsible and impossible sky, that collection of particles that is defined by its distance from the plant, blue and bluer with the extended expanse from tendril or leaf to impossible blue, though he was not a plant and could not grow in time or grasp his wife's hand, could not move his feet, could not use the sunlight that started to leak through the curtains to extend himself forward and though he loved her more than anything in the world, finally, the sea had its say and she collapsed right where she stood, and

still overcome with panic and waiting for the burst of
courageous adrenaline that might push him to react
accordingly, he had been unable to lurch forward and
instead, had stood there still as the screams escalated,
then stopped, even as the rain continued, and as he
surveyed the room, his legs slowly crumpled and gave
way and when the morning came he was there on his
knees quietly sobbing, his wife's body an untraversable
distance away, like the sky, like the sun, like the rest
of the cosmos. They had been visiting the coast for her
benefit, the salty air gave her purpose, she claimed, but
after the storm finally subsided he packed up only what
he could carry in his one piece of luggage and returned
home. He grew paranoid of the inability to predict
the goings-on inside the human head, how could one
prevent a wound or illness such as this when there
were no outward symptoms, no data to be interpreted
or observed. Everything had been fine. She had been
fine. And then —

His mother had not approved of her, though most
likely she would not have approved of anyone her son
brought home short of an empress, and yet, even then,
she might have rambled on about the entitledness or
excess of regality, the slight tinniness of her voice —
the standards she kept impossibly high for her son
would have a certain effect on his egoistic dealings and
reigned silences as he would constantly work to justify
the vast thoughts and decisions made around him and
attempt to live up to the icon that his mother had built,
though he admired her and the elegant manner with
which she was able to carry herself, her stately posture,
her always-perfectly-symmetrical bun, her capability
to have remained standing after the multiple storms
that had tried to knock her down, she stood erect and
regal, like a tall and wise redwood, while on the other

hand, he bent easily with the wind—adaptation, he
told himself—like the palm trees in this great desert
city that signaled the direction of the winds, or past
winds, even when there was no breeze left to be felt,
just the ashy air and beautiful, magnificent sky, the
sky of perpetual burning, earned only by the cruel and
unyielding destruction, as the most beautiful sky one
could possibly encounter. It was the kind of renewal
most humans had learned to fear: a complete one, and
of course any dreamer that engaged with the process
would be naive to believe they might be included in
the time after. For anyone who breathed this air in
this place, there was no time after, just time, and not
much of it. What he regretted most was the way his
family had treated his wife, and he had wondered if her
place in the hierarchy of things was what really had
dissuaded her from having children. *What kind of proper
wife can't provide her husband with children,* his mother
would admonish. *Not can't, Mother, won't. And the decision
is mutual. I don't want to bring children into this world either.*
And his mother would roll her eyes, sigh in frustration,
and continue to complain about his wife's inability to
cut fruit properly, her indecent fashion, the way she
wore her hair (in a perm, shoulder-length, with bangs
that fell over one side of her face, *like a starlet,* he used
to think), and his wife would take it, serve everyone tea
and clear their plates as if she had somehow subsumed
the role of the servant, and no one would say thank
you, and neither would he, and only later would he
realize what a snub that really was, how little he could
have done to help her so much.

The old man's ragged eyes are more ragged than
normal today, and though the mountains call to him
through the windows, the clouds block his view of
their majesty, though of course those are not clouds

in the distance but beautiful entrails of smoke, the
blue escape now having deteriorated completely and
only the filtered light coming in through the density
of particles and ash that signifies the loss of mobility,
an alley of symbols; it was his wife who had kept the
house in order, who had kept their schedules aligned
and their meals prepared. When he returned to their
house after her sudden death, he was thrown into a
series of endless struggles, and all he could imagine
was the menacing and threatening shore of the ocean,
as if he were trapped on a large rock a small distance
from the coast, the rock itself covered in slick and wet
seaweed, troops of barnacles cemented on the sides,
the rock surrounded by other jagged rocks, and every
time the waves crashed upward he felt the force of the
entire ocean beneath his feet and each and every time
he would feel one of his legs slip and his foot dangling
for a second over the brackish water and he would
somehow find his footing only to await the next tidal
wave, the whole of his identity somehow grappling
there within those crashing waves, and because
love's failure was not the long and empty road ahead
alone but the denial of his fate, he thought only of
the distance between things, between everything and
everyone he had ever known, the distances growing
and shrinking and growing again, and he just a weed
in the dirt, unable to traverse any distance, unable
to grow without stealing, unable to become *more*
without feeling like *less*. He hadn't known how to run
a household, given that the household had shrunk
to a number of one, he still realized that he hadn't
learned where things were stored, the location of the
sesame oil, where the extra toothbrushes were kept.
He didn't wear a watch (she had always been the one
to wake him up each morning for work, had packed his
lunches, had attended to his appointments and outings,

had reminded him of meetings with colleagues and organized their itineraries) and so with an inability to sense the passage of time from the position of the sun or the quality of light coming in through the window at any given time, he would forget to eat (the actual feeling of hunger would elude him for some time, and though loss of appetite is a common symptom of grief, the mere mention of certain dishes would cause him to break down crying, leaving well-meaning visitors or friends speechless, confused, and then finally, silent, as it was easier to leave him alone rather than to stretch the formalities of "paying one's respects" to actually trying to resolve any of his deep-seated issues, *there are therapists for that,* someone might respond to a particularly long and rambling monologue), sit in front of the television for too long (it was where he felt most at home, in distant places without actually having to travel anywhere—that had been her passion—and he found the view of things more advantageous, more consistent), and then, eventually, hours passing this way, he would find himself in the dark, all of the lights off (he hadn't touched a light switch in years), a slight grumble in his tummy, and he would look into the darkness, and the darkness would look back at him, so he would continue to sit there in the dark: disoriented, hungry, alone. His hygiene suffered as well, as, either from lack of motivation or intentional ignorance for social expectations, he would go days without showering, only putting on proper clothes when he had to leave the house for cigarettes or coffee. Mostly, he simply aged.

On one afternoon, the old man (who was not so old yet) watched a TV documentary about Étienne Bottineau, who in the eighteenth century rose to fame by being able to predict the appearance of ships a long way from shore by studying the horizon line. Inventing a new science, nauscopy, his ability to see traveling ships at a distance of almost one thousand miles from the coast without the support of radar or telescope was translated into a science of rigorous observation, though the emanations he claimed to see and their meterorical effects were unsatisfactory to many, just as the coining of the term telepathy by Frederick W. H. Meyers would be dismissed by authorities as pseudoscience or superstition. Though the old man had never been superstitious or one for supernatural beliefs, his wife had eminently believed in presences and emanations and resonances and all the possible possibilities of life and its reincarnations, and thus it was the possibility of generating such an intimacy with distance that pulled him out of the quagmire of grief, and imagining himself on the coast, his wife's hand in his hand, the salty air swirling around them with the cool breeze and the two of them barefoot and content, he imagined how she would describe the distance between themselves and the horizon line, how she would describe the distance manifested by air and the color of the sky itself as possible only by this unnavigable distance. *Blue is the color of that distance,* she would say. *And even between people, we can feel at a distance.* And she would push his hand away and walk a few feet in the opposite direction, leaving him looking a little disconcerted, trying to smile and maintain his stance where she had left him, and she would hold up her hand, close her eyes, feel the wind passing through her fingers, and smile, simply stand there and smile, her hair swirling around her face, strands of it pulling taut across her cheeks then moved aside again by the wind, and though he didn't believe her at the time, he knew that the night she had died he been unable to act, unable to reach her body, unable to access her pain, and when she had needed him most, he had been unable to accept the significance of distance, to comprehend its gifts and its curses, and watching the tide roll in and out, his eyes fixed on the screen, he thought he could maybe feel her now, could understand the significance of all the different kinds of emanations from the earth's magnetic field, from the various densities of rocks and sand and water, from the currents of liquid and air, and in an attempt to regain order over his life, he would begin to reorganize the entire house, each cupboard and closet and box of unopened relics, he would upend it all to somehow find her again, tucked away in some corner or pocket, any way to travel some part of that distance that he had been unable to on that stormy night. He didn't know how else to cope, how else to keep things in order the way that she had, and because he couldn't sense the residue in the air, the meterorical effects as waves that rode out and around him, he cleaned and organized and created new footholds for himself throughout his home, partially hoping that maybe the disturbance of all of these objects might bring back her ghost; he would have preferred to encounter her ghost as an angry and vengeful entity rather than not at all, but of course he didn't really believe in ghosts and hauntings (that was for children, he still firmly believed) and so she never appeared to him in any form, and he was never able to find her in the nooks and crannies of their once-shared home, and in his attempt to keep her from disappearing, after hundreds of iterations of reorganizing the house and dismantling and re-mantling all of the parts and items of the space, she did finally and completely disappear, many of her items donated or discarded, some intentionally and some because he no longer recognized their value (he wasn't sentimental and didn't understand attachment

to objects, *just things, they were just things,* he could
hear himself recite) or because they didn't fit into
the organizational systems he had created, and she
would not have recognized the house even if she had
returned now, the house arranged and rearranged so
many times, and eventually he would crawl back to
his place in front of the television, still finding time to
fulfill his duty to order, but anchored in that spot in
front of the bright and moving image — mesmerizing,
comforting, warm — and he would stop thinking about
her, would forget her face, would forget the feeling
of her hand in his hand, would forget the ocean air
and breeze, their footsteps on the sand, would forget
his loss and sadness, her screams and pain, would
forget each and every argument, each and every smile,
would forget that he ever had a wife, had ever been
in love, had ever held everything in his arms only to
lose it all, would forget what and that he ever had lost.
Perhaps it was just easier this way, or maybe this was
just how memory worked. In either case, here he is
today, the threatening shore a distant memory and the
vast and blasphemous ocean roaring and contained to
the confines of the television screen. He has already
fallen asleep, is already snoring, is already dreaming
and in some other place. Perhaps tomorrow he would
remember something more. Or perhaps tomorrow
he would finally slip, his leg dangling over the edge
of the sea and he would welcome the fall, the being
swallowed-up by the darkness because it wasn't death
he was afraid of, but the solace and loneliness in the
living in the wake of its fear.

18. THE WRITER

What she remembered about their final encounter
was the face he held, the expression with his drooped
eyelids, eyes wide open, mouth slightly ajar, as if
mimicking a confused child who has just had his ice
cream taken away, something he had not earned in
the first place and had cheated to obtain, the kind of
entitled pain when one has always had an audience
for these kinds of sensitivities and desires, the exact
same face he had made when she had once, jokingly,
called him cruel after he had, in turn, joked about
the disappearance of the old man who lived in their
building and speculated on whether the old man had
finally turned into one of those pigeons he was so
obsessed with, the exact same face that indicated to her
how hurt he was by the very gesture of her being hurt
by his actions, as if he couldn't possibly imagine what
he could have done to ever hurt her, and how she could
have the gall to accuse him of causing her any pain,
when all he wanted was to make her happy, to make
her feel loved, to make her love him.

Of course, it wasn't a trial of any sort that she was
interested in, just the strange pull — *what is the distance
between two people*, she wondered — of presence becoming
absence, and then, absence becoming presence in the
same way that in the imaginary intimacy with death,
the melancholic desire for justice, there is only a

suspension of judgment from the raised altars around the scattered pivot points, and why did the tears come so readily now (there was the sound of someone playing a violin coming in through the window), why did she act so predictably and childishly?

Can I assume that anything is different, that anything has changed between us? Because it hasn't, has it?

She had a desire to punish him, a kind of performed enactment of the stubbornness of relationships and the kind of cruelty she wanted inflicted upon him, so that he would *learn, realize, know* the kinds of cruelties he was capable of inflicting upon others, but she knew that such a performance would mean nothing, would improve nothing, as the sentence against a man is only the indignation of a range of tortures to be performed while alive, and to be manipulated symbolically after death, the body that even the children must watch and be punished for, this is the "beyond" of an unintentional principle of execution, the "beyond" of the perfected blade that only knows to bring a fresh breeze on the filthy neck and a weight of great sorrow. The thing was, she could see his body up there, with a sack over his face, or bent over like a donkey about to be fucked from behind, or kneeling with his hands tied behind him, or even standing with some semblance of regality and honor, and really all she could think about was the feeling of his hands on her neck, her trying to scream and trying to get away inside of her own home, his continued insistence that he *loved* her, and in the wicked fantasy of tribulations, she imagined that he really did.

The body of a great redemptive power only resonates when attributed a sort of anti-martyrdom, an involuntary mode of sacrifice, and she wanted to take

that opportunity for redemption away from him most
of all, she wanted this to be, on his part, a cowardly
act of guilt or solemn attrition, the decapitation (in
the performance of an execution), as an example of
the kind of portrait a repressed man might paint, the
impure blood and waters that mix into descent and
connect a blood-woven tapestry of a traitor, that is,
the great traitor is called such by those that retain a
sacrilegious fascination with obeying, that is, a studious
refinement of a crime that raises the soul a certain
number of inches; nothing is irreparable. And yet, *had*
he betrayed her? Had any crime been committed?
What was the pain that she was really responding to,
and how far had she penetrated the sphere of influence,
or, why, for all of her life, had she always had a strange
and consistent affection for the desert?

What she really felt in this moment was despair, but
too, she knew that the body's uncontrollable shaking
and sobbing was a sign that it wanted to live.

Too, there was a reason why she hadn't yet revealed
what her manuscript was about to anyone, including
herself.

She had never been to the desert, though perhaps
all of the land was drying up now and even this city
that had once been great and flourishing was slowly
being covered with a layer of dust that only seemed
to grow thicker and wiser. She wasn't sure where the
affection came from, what the seductive appeal was.
She didn't like heat or dryness. What she imagined
was a breath, *the* breath, heavy and achieving an
amplitude so that if she stood there, in the center
of it all under the open sky, the clouds in a field of
force under the blue sky, there was a marker of long
duration, the lore of faraway places and overnight

stays, one and the same. Perhaps it was the sky itself, a new kind of beauty in what was vanishing, in the line, itself, how the horizon contained the hope of legible communicability, the earliest symptom of kinship, of sunrise: the corresponding experience in the embrace, head-to-head, the nod of kins, precursors to all of *this*, and all the way to the horizon one could imagine this inadequacy, the atmosphere of blue, or retellings. She was always looking up, she realized (was it because of how her mother had died?) and saw somehow that the sky, everything above her, all of that lingering atmosphere was a tether to her past, and that instead, here in this city of cracks and fading moss, and because she was afraid of everything that slithered and lived below, she knew that this was what she needed to confront, the land itself, the below, the final lowering of the head, as if a last nod to her sleeping brother, an attempt to mute out the creaking under the floorboards at night, this was what she needed to face in order to have a future as herself / not herself.

She could hear the call of Genghis Khan (in a television depiction she had once seen): *Every corner beneath the Blue Sky is ours for the taking,* and though she had imagined her future self wandering in the desert for so long, she knew she had a different kind of encounter she needed to make, in order to learn something that she didn't already know about herself, and in order to be able to speculate past the framed desire of this particular present.

I don't understand, he had said.

The point isn't to understand, she had responded.

She had a greater relationship with cruelty, with finality, with the cruelty of finality, and as if triggered by his stubborn mantra of *I don't know what you're talking about,* she remembered finally how they had ruined her forever, and why severely though perhaps justly, she had continued to believe that this is why she was broken, why she couldn't be loved, why she didn't deserve to be loved, including, by herself.

She clambered around the streets; the dog was waiting for her at home, but she didn't know how to get there yet. She kept asking herself if she would be all right now, now that he had left her alone, would she be all right now, until she realized that she had heard her screams before, not her own, but similar, identical even, and she thought back to the one memory she had worked hardest to keep buried most of all, all of them out in the woods that night, her new family and other members of the church, and there had been a roiling fire and a small girl laying on a stone slab, but she had not kept still, nor silent, she was screaming, all of her limbs flailing out and then, in between her insufferable screams, other sounds came through her lips that did not sound like they should belong to a girl or any human or any creature living under the dominion of a benevolent God, and she had been there as a witness, *here is how we must sacrifice in order to maintain our course, here is how we must flush out the demons to keep our souls clean,* and she had felt rooted there in the shadows and among the trees while the adults moved around the other girl gesticulating and deciding and that girl, who appeared to be almost the same age as she who was watching from between the shadows and protection of the trees, was in no position to retaliate and all any of them wanted was to make it all stop, and there were screams, more screams (at this point it was not clear which girl was screaming), and she had wanted to go home, away from this place where girls could be possessed by demons and well-meaning adults couldn't save their children, no one could, because that is what she learned about the world that night, that there is no way to control the tickings of finality, of who gets taken or gets to live, of who is consumed and who does the consuming, there is only the will to keep going, the endlessly admired trait of survival (but too, she realized, survival was not and could not be a justification for any of it, that survival at the cost of killing was the lowest form of continuance, and because a survivor knows of many deaths and has seen many around him fall, that is the price to be paid, the banishment of harm in an effort to create invulnerability that becomes a callous, the integration of primordial abandonment and pure rage), and when they had all decided that the girl could not be saved in this way, and too, they needed to save themselves, each other, a deep-throated man read off a set of instructions and the rest of them silently obeyed, did what was needed to be done (*she is possessed, has already been possessed, we must return her to God*, they justified), and after it all she knelt with the rest of them by the river washing her hands and the feeling that suffered her entire body was so terrible that it never went away completely, just subsided into a different kind of terror, the sleeplessness, the inability to move at times, and here in the streets she understood why she felt so much like a corpse, rotting and ambling in the heat, and her face filled with horror, as if she had suddenly aged, and she tried to take one more step toward home but her legs simply wouldn't move and then, trying to shake her leg free nearly lost her step but instead of falling, knelt down there in the street and stared at the ground, short of breath, whispering something even she could not understand, and thought that maybe the pain that had stayed with her all this time was not actually the guilt or nausea of the horrific act she had been an accomplice to, but, in fact, whatever had possessed that other girl had been passed on to her now, and whatever it was that they had all wanted to get rid of so intently, that it might have been growing inside her all this time; *was she possessed,* she wondered, was she in fact, *a lost cause,* and was there anything else she would remember that had been buried, that was now to resurface to remind her of who she really was—indeed, who was she, really, and what was she becoming?

19. THE DOG

What they don't understand often is that it's not just about survival. It couldn't be. A perpetual investment in survival would be the desire to exist for always, and I understand this isn't the order of things, there is no capacity for always, just the becoming that is bracketed by the first and final breaths. Survival makes an enemy of everyone, but none of us are interested in that. We like to make bonds. This is the becoming I am interested in, while careful not to let the other dissolve completely, I am here for you as well, for them, for her, for us. What's important to remember is that it's not the loss of the dead when they are forgotten by the living, it's the loss of the living to have forgotten.

You can sense what someone is afraid of by looking at their eyes. Cats, of course, project worlds this way, and sometimes they distort the fields, humans are susceptible to this, their heads spin, and don't understand what they are being guided towards. Chickens are misleading, you can only see half of what they see at a time, and they can use this to their advantage. Of course, smell is what helps me think. Smell is often and pervasive and it fills a space evenly. There isn't deception in smell. In either case, I'll look you straight in the face. I'm smelling you but I won't miss eye contact. You might refuse to answer. But I know what has happened, even if you say nothing did.

20. THE PHOTOGRAPHER

He didn't believe in UFOs but wished that he did,
to have that idealistic connection to the nonexistent,
the kind of tether and hope on wisps of evidence
that might allow him to have more certainty in other
aspects of his life — he had read a great on the anatomy
of the phenomenon of belief, the cases made for the
inadequacy of language in the past to describe UFOs
as such, and that perhaps even the prophet Ezekiel's
vision had been of an unidentified flying object — but
he wasn't easily dazzled by the scant evidence or bright
lights and he was too skeptical, too apathetic for belief,
it required too much effort to have faith in anything,
even when the dots had been connected for him, and
mostly things would stay undecided unless some
catalyst pushed him out of that neglected corner or he
was struck by the force of something, an actual strike
of lightning, a punch to the gut, a laser, that proved to
his body its existence through the exertion of physical
force upon his body by something that was, in his
mind, tangible, and therefore real.

What he did know was that he couldn't stay here.
Somehow he had reached the tipping point where
staying in this city was no longer just a matter of
following the status quo, but rather, like a leaky pipe
that is detected only by the amount of moss that has
grown around its perimeter, the other inhabitants

had been trickling outwards, and though he had
stayed mainly to avoid having to justify any decision
or organize himself enough to make to leave (where
would he go?), he now realized at some point the
number of people who had left the city outnumbered
the number of people who had stayed, and as one of
the few remaining holdouts, he had inevitably and
unconsciously articulated the decision to stay, and this
he couldn't abide by, especially when he realized the
decision to stay had been made for him by her—the
fantasy of the two of them had grown quickly, like a
virus, and for a brief stint he really had imagined what
life for the two of them, together, would look like, him
making breakfast for her in the morning, the wonderful
mundanity of life when not alone, when the quietness
of the spirit can then dwell on other things, and with
his emotional spirit supported by the kindness of her
heart, he could become the artist he knew he could
be, great and brilliant and as yet misunderstood,
and knowing that behind many great men there had
been those even greater women to uphold them, to
contribute the necessary emotional labor of keeping
their men sane and fed and unneglected, and he had
seen, before she did, that she was capable of being
that kind of great inspiration—but now that he no
longer had a tether (was someone outside shouting?),
an anchor to hold him here, he was free to join the
tenuous current of followers and to make his way
outside where the rest of the world awaited his arrival.

There was, of course, the irresistible impulse to stay,
but he couldn't fathom staying for her or for making
any gesture that could be misunderstood by an external
witness as being done *for* the benefit of someone
else and not himself (he would not be perceived as
weak, though of course he believed in the damage of

patriarchy, the dangers of investment in masculinity
as a force for power, he had always seen these as
other people's problems, that is, he had always acted
with as much compassion as he could, understood the
vantage points of the weak as he himself understood
the inflictions of abuse and abandonment so
empathized deeply with anyone who felt marginalized
or disempowered; he also understood the importance
of individualism; he was his own person, and this
is, in the end, what would redeem him: his undying
devotion to his own humanity and more importantly,
his understanding of how the world was divided into
two categories, those who could be saved, and those
who couldn't, and he believed firmly, that he fell into
the first category, though of course anyone who saw
the world as a system that so neatly fell into binary
terms — though he would never admit this, didn't
believe in binarism or polarization, just the conscious
effort to understand and be compassionate — was
doomed, had already been falling, slowly, and probably
was already swimming in the eternal purgatory that
they would come to inhabit for some time), especially
one who didn't love him and who didn't deserve his
love or even his scorn, and though he insisted to
himself and anyone else who might listen that he only
wished the best for her, that it just hadn't worked out
between the two of them — some people just aren't
compatible and sometimes love is just not enough to
keep the bonds between people intact — he couldn't
forget the sight of her face, that look she gave him
once, that look she had on her face as she looked back
at him, her eyes open and somehow revealing that her
heart was open too, and he had wondered in what way
was her heart connected to her eyes and in that brief
glimpse of openness he had fallen more profusely in
love with her, the vulnerability of her glance piercing

and intoxicating, and he had thought that if he only
tried hard enough he could elongate that moment with
her into eternity, could make her see what he saw, and
he could continue to see the world through those same
eyes together (he did believe in redemption after all,
that there could be a tangible reward for working hard
enough to improve oneself, and with the fervor of a wet
towel, he did believe in the actuality of his principled
compassion, that even with the apathy he held he could
aim to treat others the way they deserved to be treated,
as humans, as living beings, and he thought that if he
could only take care of her in the way she deserved, he
might be rewarded with her companionship, no, with
her love, and that was all he had ever wanted from
life), and the recitation of words out loud would only
break the spell so he had said nothing, only stared, and
she had looked away, embarrassed, and then, she had
never looked at him that way again.

He could say he was staying for himself, and to that
effort would probably have to compensate for his
own doubts on whether he was capable of making
any decision for himself without repeating this fact
to all of his neighbors, to anyone who would listen,
but there was no one left to have to prove himself to,
and besides, he was insisting on enough simultaneous
directives already and as he had an insistent identity to
uphold, he felt increasingly anxious and pressured, and
felt that maybe this was some kind of crisis, the crisis
of the urgency of trauma—shuddering—or the crisis
of the myth of freedom, of the agreement they had
made to protect each other, the crisis of the persistence
of breathing, heavily—breathing—the crisis of the
nothing, the darkness, the terrifying memory of
the ill-revealed, the crisis of almost being there, to
a destination, the crisis of elliptical submergence—

shaking—the crisis of the insistence of staying here in this city, the crisis of time—breathing heavily—and realized he was emphasizing his own expulsion (*expulsion* seemed more appropriate than *fleeing*), so that he was in that familiar state of being acted *upon* and not as a wretched beast who follows a certain scene, rather with this kind of intrinsic exclusion he could cling to his ideals and carry the burden of his body outward, sober and steadfast.

He would go to the desert, not because that is where she had always talked about, but because he knew she would never leave, would never actually make it there herself, and because it was the penultimate stop on the train (he couldn't bring himself to reach any end, he wanted an option always to go further, to continue forward, and he was not ready for any inkling of finality yet), and with the heat of the city, the sweat already dripping down from his brow, it seemed a natural progression to collaborate with the climate's own burgeoning, to push himself to adapt to the world's own natural evolution—as if this were part of the world's natural progression, its own bodily functions as symptomatic of aging, as if he believed that planets had hot flashes or went through menopause like women, the earth was female, after all, wasn't it?—and he embraced the challenge, was energized by it even, and proceeded to pack his things.

The question was, did he care about mere survival? He was convinced that he wanted to do better—the desire to *be better* isn't almost ever a genuine one and the weeds, for example knew the dangers of giving in to that kind of delusion, as if there is a spectrum of morality that humans can move along, an axis of performance and improvement (humans are indeed obsessed with *improvement*)—but he hadn't given himself the space for that kind of continuity, rather he had assumed he was a changed and learned person trying to do better within the confines of who he was as a person already, and he had dismissed the real notion of growth and though a mythical creature in the woods might have advised him, the weary traveler, that he needed new eyes in order to continue his quest as the tragic hero, he didn't know where to get them and did still believe in the kinds of endings so many books and films offered as a kind of penance for those impatient souls, wringing their hands and darting panicky glances while avoiding any kind of real self-examination, the reflection in the mirror only as a kind of advertisement to settle into.

As he scanned his apartment, evaluating each object's potential value or significance to him in this next leg of his life, he hesitated on an overturned photo covered in dust, which upon flipping over to its proper side, there was an image of a bird: clear, vibrant, alive—this photo had been his grandmother's favorite, just a test shot of a bird on the windowsill after she had scattered some birdseed—and though the photo was blurry, out of focus (for him, he had misjudged the focus, made an amateurish mistake), his grandmother had deemed the image beautiful, deliberate and holding an artistic foresight for which she declared that she was proud. The colors bled together, and she had loved the strange quality of light that illuminated the bird's head, as if in flight, as if thinking, as if in the middle of his own artistic process.

It's like a self-portrait. Caught in mid-brilliance.

He wasn't sure of how he felt being compared to his own mistake, but she had been so certain of the image, and of him.

She had had the photo framed and hung on the wall
over the fireplace, but later, when her memory would
begin to fail, she wouldn't recognize the image, would
complain about the piercing glare that the incoming
sunlight would cause, and she would repeatedly ask
him to close the blinds or to move the wretched thing,
and though he knew her state-of-mind was not her
own (and yet it was), he couldn't help feeling viciously
hurt by her rantings, and one evening, holding back
tears, would take the framed photo and drop it into
the dumpster behind the building. The next morning
though, he would encounter the image hanging in its
old spot on the wall. His grandmother would deny
having rehung it, but that was where the framed photo
would reside until the day she died. Immediately after
he returned home from the hospital, and upon crossing
the threshold of the apartment, he would see the bird
staring back at him, like a distorted mirror, and unable
to live with himself in that state, he would take down
the frame, remove the photo, and leave it face down on
the mantle until he had forgotten about its existence
altogether.

He gazed vacantly at the photo for a long time, the
photo becoming heavier in his hand, and the dust
sticking to his fingertips, to his sleeve, and he took a
deep breath that might have indicated some kind of
resolution or complete thought around the image, an
implication of making peace with one's past through
a resurfaced relic, but he hung there, like the over-
ripened figs on the tree outside that had been dropping
each day onto the sidewalk, cooking in the blasted
heat, the smell of rotting figs as tenacious as the figs
that would stick to the bottom of one's shoes and
he thought to this morning when he had opened his

computer to discover the word-of-the-day (he had
subscribed to the service in yet another attempt at
general improvement), which was *andragogy: the methods
or techniques used to teach adults*, and for some reason, he
had felt offended, as if being caught while undressing
with the window wide open, and this is the word he
pictured in his mind while holding that image of the
bird, his arm weary and his hand weakening its grip,
and of course the question of language is absolutely
useless, futile, the salty taste in one's mouth when the
devil is at your beckoning, when you are God himself
(isn't that every artist's real and honest fantasy?)
and someone is being killed in every instant of this
testimony: fatal, inevitable, vanishing, and he couldn't
see beyond the bird where out *there* people were being
born and people were dying and in here his hand was
heavy, and out there people were vanishing and in
here he felt like a diminished man, too worried and
too tentative to make any damn difference to anyone.
He imagined them out there, the deserters that would
be trampled or those that would choose not to flee,
abiding in the instances of their own deaths while
birds dropped dead from the trees, if only to maintain
order, to stay for order, delayed and recovering some
continuous succession of the real, though he knew that
he wasn't loyal to anything that large, he could only
attest to a betrayal that had gone on already, and yet,
anything can change, he thought, anything can change.

21. THE BEARS

In another world, the bears and the trees share dominion over their planet. Their language is branching and encompasses tangents and cycles, like the migration of trees and the thought patterns of living beings that hibernate and know that time is circular. Here, the plants remember their purpose, even if others have forgotten.

A famous bear poet aphorism: *Being unto existence / Existence unto us all / Us all unto being.*

Of course the trees have always reached for the stars, and here, the waters are abundant with salmon. The trees have a cosmic perspective because their own life is intimately linked to the stars, and because both trees and bears hibernate, the landscape knows balance and we can imagine a world where the vantage point is of reciprocity rather than control.

22. THE OLD MAN

On the morning of the eclipse, the old man is visited
by a cat. He does not get along with animals and he
does know how to react, how to respond, or what to
do. His inclination is to do nothing, to ignore it, and as
with most things, the mewing will eventually stop and
the cat will eventually leave and he can get back to his
routine — today he has already been distracted from
his previously prioritized task of sorting his mother's
clothes, which he has kept all of this time in large
trunks and suitcases and boxes, and upon seeing a red
stain on a silk white blouse, felt himself deranged and
imagined her slipping on the blood-stained kitchen
tile, here the slipperiness of the splattering more
disconcerting than the color or the source — but this
morning he feels that he is losing the memory of his
mother's voice, tinny and leaden, and his gaze flits
from the table to the window and he can still hear the
mewing and suddenly he recalls his mother's voice
insisting (she would adopt a particular tone of silvery
insistence when she wanted him to eat something,
to turn off the light, to fetch her medicines, or even
to read her the close captions on the television with
the volume muted), and so he opens the window a
little, peeks his head out and waits for the creature to
approach. *Your move,* he thinks, as he is new to this,
interacting with animals, that is, and there it is again,
the voice of his mother *(Time to wake up!),* though he

is already awake, and he feels that he has undertaken something significant at her behest. The cat jumps inside without trepidation, takes a bite out of his lunch (he had been eating cold rice and beef stew, the same as his mother used to make for him but he had never paid attention to the recipe so this was a clunky mimicry at best), and then stands, tail erect and behind at a slight angle, its head turned back to look at him expectantly, and wanting to fulfill the creature's expectations, he reaches out to pet the cat, feels the cat arch its body into his palm, guiding his hand along its spine and back up along its stiffened tail, and when the cat is satisfied with this one long trembling stroke, swats some of the rice off his plate onto the floor, looks back at the man's open mouth, then leaves the way it came in. What the old man does not remember is that he had a wife: this is the memory that he has most successfully hidden from himself, even all of her belongings have become assimilated into the forage of everything else, or discarded in those fits of difficulty, and though he remembers being in love —often he thinks to himself, *I was in love once, but that was a long time ago* —he is unable to conjure up her image anymore, rather, he has somehow replaced one unbearable loss with a bearable one. He had been dependent on his mother, yes, but that dependency would ebb based on the kind of situation he was in, that is, he didn't know how to move past loss the way other humans did, and would, in any extreme emotional state, revert back to childish leanings and run back to his mother. His mother had always been the anchor, though her death hadn't traumatized him like the death of his wife had, he had manipulated the mapping of her influence and created a different, more manageable trajectory of mourning for himself. Like in pruning the pea plants outside, he relied on a kind of morphogenetic memory, influencing the shape and form of his future. In botany, it is the existence of the apical bud, the topmost one usually, that inhibits new growth on the lateral buds. But if the apical bud is cut off, it removes that inhibition, and the lateral stems can grow outward, reaching sideways and creating new pathways. He hadn't been able to live with his wife's death, the memory and knowledge of that loss wasn't just traumatic, it had inhibited him in all manners and he had been paralyzed. He thought about the structure of a traumatic experience, that is, an experience like being pricked or wounded, and how that pain causes one to act differently, to have that traumatic memory affect future actions. The definition of a traumatic memory, he thought, was simply one that influenced future action in a negative way. A traumatic wound was a wound that was considered to be disturbing precisely *because* it influenced the future. It was terrifically complicated, he had believed, that if he were to have to react perpetually in response to a particular trauma, he would frame the original trauma differently, and somehow, with a belief in the possibility to change the expectancy in the *heart* of things, to change the shape of his wound and loss and therefore the shape of his future into one he could live in, he erased the memory of the only person he had ever loved, had ever really cared about, had ever given him a reason to live past the default state of mundane existence, that is, though he may not have possessed an actual drive to live, he did so anyway because it seemed like the proper thing to do.

He hears the mewing again emanating from the small space under the awning outside the window, but feels he has done enough, shuts the window with a gusto, and allows his humanity to dissolve like salt in the ocean and living in that zone of lingering, lingering on nothing, he feels small and faraway, fading into the horizon line like a speck and in the end, that's all he is, another flitting dust mote falling slowly, meandering in the open space of the room with the air current and then eventually settling in the corner of the windowsill where dust rags often neglect to penetrate and here, he is comfortable, able to think again, able to rest.

The old man (how old is he really? for though he has the knowledge of his own age embedded somewhere in the folds of his cerebral cortex he works diligently to suppress the surfacing of this piece of data, not for the fear of being reminded of how long he has left, but for the reminder of how long he has already lived) thinks of orchards, wonders if the apricot orchards he remembers running through are now just part of a dream or if he ever really lived there—had he really lived somewhere with so many trees in their orderly rows, planted there by darkly tanned men, and he a pale boy running in and out of them, zigzagging between branches and plucking ripe fruit off the stems, wiping his hands on his jeans—it seemed impossible now that he could have run around with that much energy, that much enthusiasm and joy, and he thought perhaps this was a mirage, (could memories be mirages?), and he remembered too the day he was walking home and saw the boy that the other kids had already sternly decided was not *one of them*, he had decided this day he would go over and say hello, find out who this kid was who walked so far to get to school and walked home so far and somehow this unattainable and collective distance allured him: this strange boy traveled everyday by foot from a faraway land, lurking in the shadows and hardly

seen, he always ate by himself at the yellow plastic
table in the most remote corner of the cafeteria, the
table that had previously only been occupied by the
"special education" students, all of whom had either
disappeared or been transferred to city schools, always
with his legs crossed and his lunch accompanying
him in a bright blue box with a tightly fitting white
lid, he was always writing what seemed like poetry in
his notebooks in math class, constantly chewing his
fingernails and always frowning, most of all, the old
man, as a boy, had especially felt he could identify with
the strange boy's discomfort in any space he was forced
to occupy, though the truth was he couldn't really
empathize, he only felt like he could, he wouldn't have
described himself as content, yet with the privileges
afforded him at his age he should have been, and still,
he was just a boy and he couldn't ever be satisfied with
what he already had and so seeing this other person
who seemed to be so remote and inaccessible and so
utterly of another place, so utterly not belonging to
this world, and there *was* something in that posture, his
sunken back and defeated nature, though he was a boy
and boys shouldn't be defeated so early and be made to
believe they might be able to conquer the world before
they conceive of the skepticism and realism of the
world—he wanted more than anything to be friends
with this other person, felt he could learn something
more about himself and so, seeing him off in the
distance, he couldn't mistake that dark hair and certain
manner of walking, slightly duck-legged, bowl haircut,
he ran down the path, and out of breath, managed,
Hello, I heard you live over by the coast, do you really walk
that far every day? and the boy, with the expression
of someone who had never heard human language
directed at him before, that odd and curiously blank
stare of a common pigeon, didn't quite know how to

answer and kept walking, as if a giant fly was buzzing around his head and if he walked faster maybe it would leave him alone, and again, *Are your parents really oyster farmers?*

Eventually the two boys became acquainted with each other, became *friends* even, though this was a complicated term within the disclosed hierarchy of their society, and the old man eventually came to know more about where the other boy came from. The boy's family lived in a remote fishing village where almost everyone was an oysterman or oyster shucker. He would describe the monumental mountains of oyster shells that surrounded the town, these heaps of discarded shells that would form strange and uneven midden, the piles that were larger than his house, larger than all of the houses in the town.

How long have they been there?

They've been there ever since I've lived there, ever since my parents lived there.

Doesn't anyone remove them? Isn't there someone to pick up the piles and take them to the garbage dump?

The boy didn't answer. He had memorized entire fleets of words and phrases, *be prepared for any response,* his parents had trained him, *we are different and will always be seen as different here,* his parents would warn, *we don't have much but we have each other, and that is more than some others have,* they would attempt to lift his spirits on hot summer days when he would stand outside under the fiery rays of the sun, the stench of oysters and dead fish as thick and dense as the piles of cracked shells they emanated from, his only companions the discarded oyster shells, these giant monuments that reached

toward the sky but would never find glory, and he
didn't know quite know how to explain the loneliness
of being part of a family that believed so devotedly in
the permanence of their situation, that they were lucky
to be here, to be doing this work, to have something of
their own, unwilling to see the hellish precarity of their
existence, and again, the same blank stare of pigeons
waiting for death, flanked on all sides by their own
miserable past and their own miserable future.

On his thirteenth birthday, the old man received
a one-hundred-dollar bill from his parents, and in
excitement, asked the dark-haired boy to join him for
"a proper meal out." They were boys, children really,
and to the old man, a fancy meal at a fancy restaurant
seemed like the pinnacle of luxury. After school the
two boys arrived at an establishment that had been
vetted and researched, and the old man's parents
(who were absent, as usual, but attentive to their son's
desires) had called ahead to let the restaurant know to
expect the two young lads and to treat them with the
appropriate level of care and attention, and as he tried
to suppress the level of excitement that was visible by
unfolding the cloth napkin and refolding it on his lap
over and over again, he tried to take the appropriate
amount of time in perusing the menu though the menu
was only a single sheet of paper and he had already
researched all of the selections the night before.

I'm going to have the potato pasta! He could barely contain
himself, and was attempting to perform the etiquette
of coming to a decision of what he might order at this
present moment to allow his companion to also decide
in this present moment, and he didn't want to influence
his companion's decision; he cared genuinely for his
new friend and had been excited to invite him to this
event as, he hoped the other felt the same way, his

best friend, but also knew that his family was poor and hoped that he would appreciate this gesture of allowing him to experience this kind of dining experience, and perhaps, afterward, they would laugh together at the waiter's intonation or kitschy lamps that dinned the interior, and then return to their respective abodes, their respective worlds, their respective positions in the stratified society, which the boys would only learn much later that no amount of school or money or male bonding would break, and no matter how much they loved each other, they would always remain an untraversable distance apart. He paused and enacted a thinking face, studying the menu with his eyes squinted and eyebrows furrowed.

I think the special sausage and rice suits you, doesn't that sound good?

The other boy nodded.

And then I thought we might share the oysters. I've never had oysters before! And then of course dessert. I think we should share the bread pudding. I hear that the chef here makes it without raisins. I just detest raisins, don't you? My mother always sneaks them into everything and claims they will help with my digestion but I just feel like I'm eating old, wrinkly things and it reminds me of getting old. I'm never going to get old, if I can help it.

The other boy, avoiding eye contact, muttered out as if about to vomit something: *I'm allergic to oysters.*

Ah, right okay. Something else then.

You should still order them. It's your birthday.

Well, okay. Maybe we will also ask for some extra bread and oil.

The other boy nodded, shifted his weight in his seat,

and returned his eyes back to the comfort of the paper menu, continued to *peruse*, exhaled deeply.

The old man had assumed that it was the inevitable trauma of the boy's own forced and intimate relationship to oysters that had prompted him to declare that he was allergic to oysters, and remembered feeling the shame of the entire situation, his arrogant impulse to *help* the other boy, on his own birthday of all days, giving the boy something special in order for him to feel better about himself, as if that was somehow a gift to himself, and he realized how ridiculous this all was. What did he know about the trauma of poor, immigrant farmers that had to shuck oysters to survive? He imagined the biblical-sized mounds of oyster shells piling up in the hot dry sun and then the arrival of a giant tidal wave that would cover the piles and the oyster shuckers and the boy, swallowing them completely and then sweeping clean the entire town, leaving behind only the stench and bubbling white foam along the coastline.

The old man realizes that the mewing has stopped. As he smells the faint smell of burning trees pushing through around the edges of the closed window, he wonders why he is still here, whether he even cares about survival. He is capable of killing, this he knows about himself as he has done it more than once before, but what does such a low gesture of survival mean in a world like this, does it mean anything to survive, to still be here, to outlast the others if he has never carved out an escape route for himself? As he catches the flicker of a dust mote in the light, he feels himself lowering the periphery of his vision, doubting what he has ever contributed to the living world in this long existence he has managed to lead, thinks about the trajectory of his entire life and all of the events that have led himself to this point, here, in this apartment, in this dying city, grieves the deterioration of his legs that are no longer reliable enough to even carry him out of the building, and remembering that he has nowhere to go, and that really, all of this started the day he was born, he remembers to breathe and answers himself with the only possible answer, *Not quite yet.*

23. THE MOSS

Here, a world of relation.

In another world, the in-between liminal states of day and night, land and water, and life and death find concreteness in the pale colors of the sky. These are certainties rooted in transition, and the creatures here know to pay attention. *Think lightly of yourself, and deeply of the world,* they repeat. The amphibians that inhabit this world know the treacheries of polarizing life and death, and so in their journeys on both land and water, still remember the invigoration of the birth of civilization itself. Here, nothing is ever forgotten or forgiven. The amphibians, as creatures that inhabit two different worlds simultaneously, immediately, naturally, and in their dependence and profound understanding of the environment, the cycles of the sun and the erosion of time, constantly ask the question of home, and know that there is no map that could outline any worthwhile trajectory.

Everywhere the moss breathes, then hibernates, then breathes. Everywhere, all of the plants and animals breathe together in an intimate cycle that is shared and just like language, can only exist *because* it is shared,

Before all of this, there was a *before* that was rooted in an ugliness, a kind of ragged contentment in difference, the distance between a body and home as equal to the kind of forbidden question, *What is home?*

Today the relational qualities of air are the relational qualities of words, and you may learn more from paying attention to what lies beneath your feet than what composes the sky above you.

24. THE WRITER

Only after she realized he had disappeared, did she too realize that she had been looking for a sign to depart, that in the light of this it wasn't a surprise that in order to rid herself of her own muddled past she still needed some kind of catalyst to take that next step for herself, to figure out a way to be alone, really alone, and to feel her own presence, her own self as a companion walking up that steep path to some kind of redemption (if that were even possible), though her dog's rampant and heavy breathing reminded her that redemption didn't exist, not for her or for anyone else, and as she focused her vision on the evening light catching the dust on the metal edge of the windowsill, the dense breathing of her dog and her own slow, steady exhale, she could visualize the slow procession on the jagged, cobblestone avenue, parts of it yet obscured, her own legs carrying her along within and inside the murmuring shadows, as slow as she could imagine walking without falling over, not from exhaustion or overexertion, but from the patient withdrawal into a focusing outward from a point, with the discipline and predilection of an orange-robed monk, her own corporeal reality as a center that connected with the infinite number of centers in the woods, each tree standing tall, listening — they preferred to listen rather than to speak — and her own mobile body navigating between the trunks and branches, breathing with them all, together, and she finally felt her panic subside into air and then, the song of a solitary bird emanating from the darkly wooded areas that was the sonic reminder of parasitic aspiration.

She realized that her own insistence and deep-seated desire to go to the desert all of her life had been like a water-drenched farewell, that is, she wanted a familiar kind of suffering that stretched out, vast and dry and endless, a place where she might be swallowed up or dry out slowly like jerky, and her body, already perfectly empty and rid of the emotional labor of productivity, could be abandoned, deserted, and she might find some residue of purity, something resembling salvation out there in the land of sand and hot winds. The desert was a certain kind of old place, a place people escaped *from* and not retreated *to*, and this was why she had been so drawn to it, the secret place of her past where she had tucked away her ghosts and perhaps they might follow her there, and with her, wither away and die once and for all.

But this was exactly why she would escape the geography of her routine now, or at least create some kind of immediate rupture by retreating to a place with very old beings, those trees of yesteryears and centuries, to learn something she didn't already know about herself. Here was her chance to acknowledge something about her tether to the past in a way that didn't feel like she was carrying around these oversized and sentimentalized loads of rocks, that is, the past up to this point had been something she had tried to forget about, that pulled her and stretched her in dispersive directions but she had always tried to make do and think on the tasks in front of her, even as she was shaking off her shoes caked in the ancient mud of her ancestors and imagining spiders in every corner of the house, the archival preservation of her own ghosts written in the auratic fragments of her own words. Sometimes the descent of one makes possible the ascent of every other.

She didn't know who her people were *(Dear mother, I'm writing to you from the inside of this place and what the language shows is how greatly we have diverged from one another, and though I miss you everyday, it is in forgetting your face that I have learned how to survive)*, though what was evident in the switching off of the great darkness and the void that surrounded our bodies was the manipulation of aura—isn't homeland just a series of sentimentalized feelings that only leads to displacement and heartbreak?—when had humans become the only people among all of the multiple persons and how did a story, excited now by the immanence of her journey, teach her to think about the future, the present being swallowed up entirely by speculation and excursion, temporary meanderings segregated into bridges, but she understood now that it wasn't that more bridges needed to be constructed but that the consciousness of the world, the breath itself, already united them all and she remembered the hawks in the sky after her mother had died, how she had been afraid to look up into the sky for fear of something long and metal piercing her skull or a stray nail falling into her eye, and she remembered that when she dared to glimpse upward there were the hawks circling, not like circling prey but in the form of a protective circle, and she remembered the ritual of gazing up at the sky every morning from her window, and because a group of squirrels is called a scurry she remembered the squirrel that landed on her arm, made eye contact with her, then launched itself off of her arm to land on a tree and scurried to meet its comrades, as confused about the detour as she

had been, and she remembered noticing the tiny green
forests beneath her feet and wondering what else she
had been stepping on this whole time, what else had
she missed, what more did she have left to encounter
in the future as an "I" because only the "I" has a
future and the other beings are left to be reflected and
deflected then vomited out on any randomly fateful
day and the warding circle carries news of wind and
the birds carry news of death and the moss carries
news of resurgence and she had prayed so hard once
for her mom to die after a silly fight after school when
she had ducked to miss the scissors that her mother
had propelled at her head in a fit of rage and then,
the next morning before school, had seen the young
chubby boy with the droopy eyebrows walk into the
boy's bathroom and then the screams that followed
after he shot himself and what they all had focused
on was where he had gotten the gun, and not why he
had felt that he needed to do such a thing and if he
were a ghost now, did he regret it, could he see us in
the heated panic of the moment, the other students
stumbling around afraid and unable to understand
anything more about each other or themselves, just
that the world was a dark and scary place and we are
sometimes pushed to take drastic actions and it isn't the
act of pulling any trigger or even holding a gun up to
your head, but an eternal and excruciating scream that
builds up in your bowels and it is so loud, so incredibly
loud and you put your hands to your ears but you
can't block out the sound, and there is no sound, just
the feeling of your own scream and the intensity of a
scream that can't escape but is felt with the rollicking
of your body and your own eyes are accomplices to
your own murder but murder implies intention, and
there is no intention in this kind of pain, in this kind
of loneliness, only the gripping tighter of the handle,

the wanting to breathe, just breathe, just breathe
again, and you feel the air start to fill your lungs and
finally an exhale that brings you back to the place of
peace, but at the moment when your breath connects
with the breaths of each and every other living being
on the planet the trigger has been pulled and you no
longer have to do the work of breathing ever again, it
has finally been forfeited, and the intimacy you tried
so hard to find in life is the intimacy you attempt to
articulate in language and though she tried to write
about anything other than herself, and though she
wasn't writing for anyone in particular, without
language she didn't know how to be close to anyone
and though he had longed to be close to her he hadn't
learned yet what intimacy really was and though she
knew exactly what intimacy was, was only stuck in the
future possibility of pain, knowing too well how much
it could hurt and so was stuck instead in the nonlinear
body of accepting the immanence of pain, and no
amount of cleaning or washing would make the blood
go away, she was, after all, alone, and that was how she
preferred it, and there was the dog, his sigh a signal
she wasn't alone, had never been alone, and she sighed
back a sigh of relief because she finally understood the
finality of breath, that is, that it wasn't final at all.

25. THE SQUIRRELS

The squirrels remember in decades. That is, while they breathe circles into the winter air, one will slip down the muddy walkway and have his spine pressed upright by a memory of running forward, dry cough and chilly wind like needles, showing up for another on a street corner in the dead of night. This isn't his memory but he recognizes the early morning vibration, the ground shaking, the sky shaking, his feet, and he knows that in order to appreciate the sun he will need to traverse the street and be elated, at least momentarily, by the unused water pooling on the side of the street.

He sees the other squirrel when the crow starts clicking, sitting atop a wire and the sun finally blazing down to proceed into day. It is day. The squirrel approaches the other, and, cheeks wriggling and butt smashing into the grass, he presses the palm of his hand into her chest and her mouth rewinds. The arms might lose themselves in dreams but the squirrels always know where they are. When one is no longer visible to the other, there is no crying but a shouldering of the post and the fullness of survival that contracts and protracts with the waning and waxing of the moon. He knows not to demand and she knows not to wait up. This comes from experience, from decades of memory. After all, if they are running in circles and up and down trees, the memories ought to loop in figure-8 patterns as well, so when creatures grind their teeth it is not only during evening slumber.

26. THE BIRDS

A bird who is an oracle steps forward and catches
that kind of rare breath that signals the possibility of
speculation, and because the bird has memory and
because the bird has sight, he is able to speculate
beyond the present, that is, the future can be
formulated via dream and crying and desire, not just
the constraints of a tethered present, and yet the other
birds don't know what to search for and can only
see below them and forward, and though as they fly
they soar above the land and trees and people and
see the cycles of greenness and war and forgery, they
don't always know how to see it all simultaneously,
at both the grand scale and the small, and the type of
narrative a bird might spin is often mythological and
encompassing and they don't yet see the need for maps
because they can see it all spread out below them and
because they have memory.

Yet another of these, a bird who has been exiled for
documenting and archiving and creating maps and
records of flight patterns and migrations and the
shapes of clouds and different species of trees, this
bird who sees value in concretizing memory to outlast
one's own life and trajectory, is also capable of being
homesick, of longing for a home that exists or could
exist because the diagrammed language is also capable
of forging a threshold between this world and the

dream world, and so that in-betweenness might be labeled as a concrete space and there might be new language manifested to articulate all that does not yet fit into the confines of current restrictions, that is, there are so many different types of knowing, and we have so many words to describe all those forms of knowing that privilege certainty and fact and truth, and yet everything else becomes relegated to feeling or intuition, as if there is a hierarchy that is predicated on certainty, and we know of course that certainty is an illusion and a framework for control, for cutting down trees, for carving out swaths of land to be territorialized on maps as evidence, for allowing some categories of living beings to have hope and for others to never glimpse the possibility of future beyond tomorrow.

Tomorrow, you will go up the mountain. Tomorrow you will sleep and you will dream. Tomorrow, you will kneel down before a tree and realize what it has given you, what you have taken, what you have received. And you will eventually hear the language of the birds and the language of the trees and you will remember what it was like before home was stripped away from you and you, on your knees, will remember how to stand, tall like the trees, eyes unfixed and seeing in all directions, especially down, because that is where things happen too, below you, and though gravity asks bodies to fall down, hope asks bodies to rise up.

27. THE PHOTOGRAPHER

One of his earliest lessons in getting along with others had also been his discovery of accommodation, that is, he had learned that assertion was very rarely desired from other humans and even if it was, it needed to be disguised in the conjugation of a sincere desire, and that the stuttering pace that he was accustomed to was too much stuttering, too much pause and hesitation, even for the perfectly wind-tossed hair he was apt to wearing, and rather, ambivalence and apathy were even more detestable, and he could see the disgusted looks on their faces when he would stand there, both hands in his pockets, back lurched over, his face sinking into his upper chest as if his neck had been swallowed up by the rest of his wallowing body, and more than anything, he didn't want to be seen as weak — he genuinely considered himself a compassionate and accommodating human being — and he could read in others' bodily gestures what they really wanted from him, so whenever there was a group decision to be made, he had become an expert at coaxing the correct decision out of the others and thus emerge as *easy-going* and *fun to be around*. Often, after being asked a question that was a bit direct or piercing, he would enact that look of being *deep in thought*, and because he didn't want to seem cowardly or avoidant, he had formulated a particularly contemplative facial expression that he would employ while instead he would be watching the shadows and patterns of leaf movements with the wind or would be measuring the distance between the speaker's eyes, and when the sound of ringing in his ears would finally subside, he would have gathered enough data about the other to produce something worthwhile, something that would acknowledge that he had *heard* them and valued them and their inquiries and place in the world and that he was someone who paid attention and put in extreme effort to understand others, and this could be seen of course by how long he could sit still with himself, only with the wind and light of the sun, only with the silence that wasn't silence at all, and they would agree that *he had a good picture of it*, and nod and say, *that's what makes him a good photographer, he's patient and can wait to see what something is really made up of*, and he would *believe* these statements and embody the certainty of his own benevolence, further connect the dots of his trajectory of how his troubled childhood had led him here, how he had *survived* and *overcome* and when he would start to feel really crazy, he knew to suppress the shame because it was only there to deter him, he was better than so many others, he could see that clearly, and again the ringing, and again the natural regard for others that allowed him to regard himself as *talented*, and though he believed this, the length of his hesitation was accumulating and mutating into some other kind of self-loathing, he didn't loathe himself, in fact he found himself a model of someone who has overcome horrible circumstances and someone who had in fact turned out well despite how he could have ended up instead, and he could of course dream up a million other possibilities for despicable archetypes that would stem from similar circumstances, and he could cross each and every one of them off the list and leave himself, clean-shaven and patient —*oh, how good a listener he was!* —and still wonder, how does one begin again, or, where did the bracketing of life come from?

He could hear coyotes howling in the daytime and with the windstorm outside, he found it confusing to interpret what the sky's affairs might say about his own. He had made it to the desert, had rented a tiny cabin near other derelict buildings and sheds and on this first morning had already seen several lizards and some kind of deteriorating dog or animal limping, perhaps wounded, through the dense brush. It was hard here to tell what was dream or reality, and in his ability to sit still, found himself sitting calmly in front of the giant window, the window almost the size of the entire wall (this was a modern cabin, everything was very white and transparent, he had felt like he didn't have anything to hide, save his enlarging belly, but he didn't like the shame of feeling shame and convinced himself that one's comfort with oneself was a redeeming quality and had already adopted walking around the house without a shirt on, anyways it was wickedly hot and he was increasingly self-conscious about the amount he was sweating, how much deodorant he had brought with him from the city, the musky odor he must have been giving off, and though he was here alone and there was no one to judge him but himself, he couldn't help but fear a potential visitor, a visitor was rare if not completely improbable, and yet he wanted to be accommodating if there was someone to come and see him, a salesman perhaps (but in this heat?) and though he was putting in conscious effort into being comfortable with his own body and odor, he was an animal after all, he understood the harsh judgment and vindication of humans and was more afraid of being cast out for something like body odor, how embarrassing that would be, and as he

started shaking from the yet-to-be-realized feeling of
embarrassment and alienation, his thoughts shifted
back to the lack of visitors, there was no one, there
was no one left who cared or knew where he was, so
the entire expectation didn't matter, and yet—) and he
sat there with his hands folded on his lap and fixed his
eyes on the reflection of the opposing / facing window
in this window, as if a window inside a window, pink
and steaming and the sun now beginning to set, and if
he fixated a little bit more he could see the reflection
of the first window in the other reflection, like an
infinite prism of windows that reflected a pinkening
sky against the desert backdrop, the growing shadows
of the brush and large reaching saguaros and he could
still hear the howling but the era of what constituted
daytime was coming to a close and just looking for
that moment when he might blink and it would all
disappear he also couldn't help himself and turned his
head toward the front door, hoping for an accidental
encounter, but he was crazy, he told himself, there was
no one to visit him and no one would come and as the
sky deepened into darker and darker shades of blue
and the darkening sky cooled the surrounding air he
continued to surreptitiously cast sidelong glances at
the door, thinking maybe she had come to apologize,
and he realized that the knocking he had been hearing
was only his own knees hitting the wooden table, he
had been shaking his legs (*You'll shake all the luck out
of yourself!* his grandma would admonish him when he
was a child) and gripped the side of the table firmly
with both hands and pulled himself up and all he could
manage to do was to walk over to the sink and pour
himself a glass of water and he downed the glass in a
manner of seconds and seeing only darkness and his
own reflection in the window now, the brightness from
within forcing him to only be able to see the interior

of the cabin reflected upon the glass, felt disgusted
with himself and his stomach and his sweaty body
and hurried to close the curtains, hurling his body
onto the bed afterward, and further disgusted with his
sensitivity to all of this, almost recoiled in shock when
he reached down to pull off his socks (why had he kept
them on this entire time anyways?) and found them
soaking in his sweat and as they popped off his feet
he could smell the odor escaping (the socks had kept
the foulness contained) and he didn't know what to
do with all of this foulness he suddenly had mounted
for himself and he did miss her but he hated her really
and mostly he didn't know how to be okay or how to
confront anything honestly and he still could hear the
howling outside, and that, at least, was a tremendous
relief.

28. THE OLD MAN

What did it mean to be proud of someone, he
wondered, not as an act of taking credit, which is
always what he had assumed, but to feel a pride that
was unrelated to a tether with the self but rather, a
genuine admiration, the rustling of denial as silkworms
in the darkness, then snapped into a silent complacency
with etiquette, and he did feel his part in this, a
contribution, an approximation or closeness, and yet,
even with all the pride he felt in that moment, he still
felt utterly and wholly outside the circle.

Had anyone reacted when the first pigeon fell from
the sky, the smell of damp rotting swirling up from
the ground to swallow the already-dead body, had
anyone fallen to their knees, heartbroken, bodybroken,
had anyone mourned or caught their face in their
own hands to sob into the sky, had anyone around
felt something beyond agony, beyond the present
moment and had been afraid for what was to come,
what the future could possibly hold now? He had
not cleaned the apartment in days, maybe weeks, and
instead, gesturing wildly with the shadows on the
wall, scratching the stubble on his chin, he had sat
at the kitchen table methodically and compulsively
cutting out the shapes of birds on various colored
papers, various sizes and shapes, the flat carcasses of
birds strewn out around his abode. As he clutched

the scissors, focused his eyes on that line between the
separation of bird and sky, felt *that* feeling, that feeling
when you see a bird fall from a tree and you can feel
your chest get tight and you can't breathe, as if you've
just lost your own child, your own tether to the future
itself, and you sense the world closing in on itself, on
you, and you notice the sky is blue and you remember
that it isn't, it hasn't been for awhile, and you witness
the loss of your own innocence, both the suicidal
and murderous tendencies that become possible, the
sincerity of a particular kind of mode for survival that
is realized, the madness of the body you were given
in birth, the madness of the body that will carry you
to your death, all of these things in the moment the
bird's body hits the ground, a soft whoosh of air that
is pushed up off the ground from the closing of space
between bird and land, here is the basis for building
an entire bias of personhood and soundless reverie for
being, here is the basis for *living* as a man, broken but
whole, hopeless but alive, an expanse of white skin
stretched out taut over a body, and he hears that slight
padded thud of the body landing, he hears it again and
again, and he continues to cut out the birds, a red bird
flying, a blue bird sitting, a green bird, a white bird,
a yellow bird, a black bird, all of the birds that, only
made of paper, were never alive, and so, can never be
dead.

He wanted to insist on the reality of their shared
ancestry, he was ecstatic and today, there was no
sun in the sky, but nor were there clouds or planes,
yet the severity of the heat persisted, even without a
visible source of the penetrating rays, and he thought,
*I may no longer be a bird, but I was once, maybe. But at
least we are both synanthropes,* and he clicked his tongue
and, in putting himself in the category of a group of

animals that was able to live from the benefit of an
association with humans and their made architectural
spaces, he had both taken himself out of the category
of *human* and made himself dependent on that same
category, and he had acknowledged the dependence
of birds on this higher life form, yet also pledged
their independence from them, and yet, what he
was really saying, was that he was stuck here, as
were the birds, in a codependent relationship with
all of these categories, the codependencies between
humans, between humans and birds, between birds
and humans, between birds and other birds, between
his own selves, and a single glance out the window
reminded him of the insufficiencies of any of his
actions, that perhaps none of this would amount
to any difference in the future, perhaps, the future
was already here, and he had already wasted away,
deteriorated, himself a mound of paper scraps, of dust,
and when the birds would congregate to encounter
their paper counterparts, they would all take off
together, feet pushing up off the ground, wings
flapping in rapid succession, and all of who he was, in
any kind of human form, all of the scraps of paper that
had ever constituted a man, would be scattered with
the wind and he would disappear forever.

It was in this disjoined state that he found himself
staring at the pile of her clothes on his bed, the few
boxes he had kept of his wife's belongings scattered
over his comforter. He couldn't help but feel that
this somehow represented his current condition, that
something about the way he constructed his inner
harmony and balance, his careful archival of grief, was
susceptible to error and could he find a way to justify
the way in which he had prolonged his own sane life by
doing away with the remnants of grief that he hadn't

been able to handle? There was the black cardigan with the embroidered flowers over the left chest, there were the black and white striped pants that she had only ever worn once but had insisted on keeping just in case they came back into style, there was the weathered and worn brown leather jacket with the giant shoulder pads, and there was the blue and yellow plaid blouse that she had worn often on outings to the beach. This was all a battle, the battle not to remember, the battle to remember, that is, he realized that he had forgotten the significance of these objects very intentionally but the inability to remember is rarely met with resignation in a human, it's natural to want to try and remember, to try and reach and fill in the gaps, and this worried him, this strange impulse to want to try and reach back into his past, and he could hear his mother, *Let the past lie. The past is where it belongs, buried.* He started at the clothes, gathered them up and put them back into the box that he had pulled them out of, taped a handwritten sign on the side of the box that read "Free," and dropped them outside his front door against the outer wall.

One thing that he had learned as a child, wandering through the fields, each season a different pattern and trajectory of crops, was the importance of weather patterns, that is, even though he had hated winter as a child, and though nothing grew (it seemed) in the harshness of winter's peak, the cold season was a necessary marker of time, a necessary arbiter for history to reset itself and a signal for the seeds buried inside of occupied ground to know when it was time to come forth again. He remembered there was a period of a few years when the winters would be warm. As a boy, he savored the warmth of the rain, the additional chances to go outside and play, the opportunity to stay out later and not freeze or get sick. But it was those years that were hardest on the farm, and his father explained to him the importance of vernalization, and how the wheat seeds needed to go through the process of enduring and surviving winter to be able to flower in the spring, that though it seemed winter was but a harsh and cruel season, there was a reason for everything, a balance even in the cycle of seasons that connected all living beings together. The old man remembered this as he walked back inside of the apartment, that necessity for enduring the difficult, that process which he had skipped in order to ensure a kind of survival that wasn't survival at all. He had forfeited his access to life *after*, not life after death, but life after life, that is, he had unintentionally used his devastation to escape the cruelty of winter and had exiled himself to a land where people did not feel sadness, of course that had been the goal, and yet, this was also a land where people did not feel happiness, and in his selfish purge, in his impulsive decision to *forget*, he had indeed forgotten why he had chosen to live at all, and this kind of loneliness, the kind where you are alone and have chosen to be alone but can't remember why and can't remember the time before, can't remember even the past moments of happiness, of sharing time with another, of being in love and of being loved, it was this loneliness that was slowly destroying him, and without the justifications of life or death, he only knew to keep going, but to where?

29. THE DOG

There is the veering in my nostrils. It's a season of death and resurrection, but what season isn't? She veers, is veering, but if she misses anybody, it is the ghost that becomes an intimate confidence. I wish she could understand how gracefully we can slide into the images of dirt here, that the mountains speak but she cannot hear them. We are all veering constantly, and to be alone doesn't mean to be dejected but still with each other. She lives by mirages, but realizing that the mirages and the everything-else are becoming each other constantly and that her reflection is constantly becoming her, just as she is constantly becoming her reflection. There are certain things I have become accustomed to. I don't know why I bite. I don't miss anybody because I don't know how, but I know what I am attached to, and that is everything. Who ever said it was easy to understand their real self? A dog, probably, but at least this is a wonderful place to be unhappy in.

30. THE FIRES

Are the fires any worse than they have been?

How does one compare scale with scale, devastation
with devastation, that is, there is a quietness of the
spirit that knows to sit with the natural cycles of
life and death but do we measure aggravation by
time, duration, or number of acres destroyed? Does
anyone emerge and advance, or stay still, do any of
our movements matter anymore? The fire is a place
for encounters and fulfillment of one's worst fantasies,
that sensation of being completely swallowed up and
consumed by the person you love, when becoming
becomes subsumed and at least the burned body then
becomes ash then becomes dust and dirt again, then
becomes something that will eventually regard those
that modulate the air, modulate visions, modulate
perspectives. Do you feel the heat? Can you breathe
steadily? When was the last deep breath you took that
didn't feel crammed with the remnants of hundreds of
ghosts, all of the perished trees and creatures that were
screaming but you didn't hear them?

How many fires are currently burning?

How many individual dust motes circle and surge
from under your feet, dazzling when struck by the
sun, the black brilliance that layers and stacks on
surfaces, concentrates of heat and more heat, where

are the lines between breath, how do we separate the air you breathe from the air that another takes in at the same moment, is the mixture of breeze a blasphemy or betrayal to purity, and when everything converges, what is the hot and blazing feeling that stirs deep within you?

How long will they burn?

Eternity, whose shredded copy is time, said Borges. That is, in another part of the country a sinkhole has swallowed a significant portion of the continent and in another an entire city has been submerged from flooding and in another it has not rained for years and the process of death is very, very slow, and mostly people do not want to panic and mostly people do not want to disturb their lives too much or too often, *We shouldn't normalize the chaos,* some might respond, so the greyness is easier to handle, the space leading up to the movement, a displacement that is made up of a series of smaller gestures and the tall trees yet stand under the low skies and tomorrow is when human life will meet its destiny.

31. THE PEA PLANT

It tucks us into the cage. Some of our tendrils reach out and they meet the surfaces they were looking for. In other parts, we feel limbs snapping off, cut off, and still we reach for hard surfaces and light. It touches us in places and sometimes this guides us to the wall, to the edges of the cage. It touches us in others, as if testing, as if making a decision about whether to let us continue to teach, to move, to become. We are always becoming and it lets us know when and where we might proceed. We only know to touch and be touched. We only know to climb and let our tips move forward and we ask to be guided because we cannot see but we can feel, we can feel every movement and coaxing and gash and pull and nip and because we are flexible we can be convinced of anything and because we want to live we can justify any of its actions for or against us, and because there is always space for one, there is also always space for two.

32. THE WRITER

This is just the way of the world, she thinks, looking down at the ground with dirt beneath her fingernails, torn between the horizontal and vertical accomplishments of her life, and wanting to shape so much of her reality via language but now understanding, maybe for the first time, that what she is participating in just by standing there between the trees and ferns and moss and lumbering branches is a kind of living and cultivation of persisting that reaches past the motion of her own life. She had finally broken the paralysis of her writing, that is, she had finally realized what she had been trying to write about, that in her circling and rewriting and extending of sentences that never ended, somehow the hesitation to end any sentence with a period linked to her own inability to push any narrative toward a sense of finality, or, like the process of squatting over a hole in the dense brush when no toilets are available and though the urge and desire are there, the strangeness of the encounter with nature in this way, that is, shitting in a hole in the woods, somehow combats any natural inclination to relieve oneself and so a person might stay in that position for awhile, squatting, legs tiring, knees shaking, until finally, one either lets it all out freely and sloppily (no one ever said taking a shit in nature was natural), or gives up, pulls her pants up, and proceeds onto the next task, and in all this hesitation embedded inside of hesitation, electrons whizzing around in orbitals and the effect of other unrelated things that still brought about concern—she had taken to cracking her knuckles over and over again, cracking her neck, even her toes, which she could now crack over and over again, the repeated pops that dotted the dark silence at night when she lay away contemplating her place in the universe, or something like that—and she realized it was the reciprocity of bodies that she was really interested in, how it was that frames of reference and relationships between and of all living beings were activated, how those activations created new conditions for increased sensitivities among others, that is, how did bodies and worlds articulate each other, how did any being's body allow another's body to affect her own, and vice versa, or, that is, how did we learn to be *affected?* She had been investigating the nuances and complications of codependencies, that is, she still missed her mother and this longing for a parent was a kind of codependency, one that was fixed and ended firmly with her own screams in the middle of the night, and she remembered all of the acts that she had been made an accomplice to, what she had been driven to do herself, an uninterrupted stream of hostility and victimhood and struggle and trauma and sitting down to write, she didn't know where one cause began and one effect ended, or if it even worked like that, and she had been listening carefully for some time, sitting here in the woods—finally she had ended up in a place that felt so incredibly foreign and yet like *home,* engulfed by greenness and air and strange interpretative embraces and something about it reminded her of an existential return to the womb (was there such a thing?)—and all of this time, without anyone to talk to except for the dog, who sighed and sniffled and rested his head on her leg from time to time to let her know that he was there, still, breathing and breathing with her, together, she realized the trees had been speaking to each other this entire time, not just to each other but to her, to the dog, to anyone who would listen, that is, not the kind of listening that involves the impatient waiting for a pause wondering, *When will it be my turn to talk?*, but the kind of listening that comes with no guarantee that you will be given any chance to respond or reply or make yourself heard, because hearing should not require a reciprocal gesture, like some some kind of distorted capitalist precipitation of communication *(an eye for an eye, an ear for an ear)*, no, rather the trees were of course listening, being affected, absorbing all of the toxins and shit that came shooting over to them, it wasn't that they *didn't* listen, it was about the lack of *expectation*, and so at its essence, her book had become a mystery novel that gazed at the relations between the trees and humans and other animals of the forest, and it was was unpublishable, probably, because of the way she had refused to use pronouns in her attempt at trying to embody the thoughts of trees and the significance of kinship without hierarchy in terms of subjecthood, and also she had come to see the sentence itself as a colonialist structure, and thought that perhaps these long sentences might be something she could give the reader, something they didn't need but would receive anyways, like a gift, like listening, or something like it, and even in all of that gesturing toward a productive contemplation that might finally lead away from the past, she wondered if it was too late for her, if in fact because of everything she had already done, everyone she had already hurt, was it perhaps too late for us all?

She was surrounded by hanging, wispy moss, spaghetti-like lichen that spooled out from the branches, so many different kinds of vegetation that

covered the bark of all the trees around her, and
she wondered how was the body of a tree different
from the body of a human, or was that even the right
question to ask?

On their first real date, he had insisted on taking her to
a small, Mexican restaurant on the other side of town.

I would drive us if we could, he said. Though they both
knew that the bodies in the street made it impossible,
and she even wondered whether he still had a car —
most people had discarded their vehicles, sold them
as scrap metal, or, without any petroleum left in the
city, the streets were packed with automobiles that had
simply run out of gas and had been abandoned where
they stood, so that the city had started to resemble the
set for a zombie movie: an overhead crane shot would
reveal what was left, which wasn't much, but was
revelatory and horrific to look at. Like the bodies that
piled up next to them, the city had started to appear
in ruins, though those that had stayed behind had
found the quickest routes and ways around the newly
materialized obstacles, and with the cars rusted, even
the pigeons didn't need them as homes (the birds, too,
a dying breed), and it was only the most resilient of
the weeds that knew to create trajectories between
the cracks and crevices of metal and flesh and grew
upwards forming giant and monstrous stalks that crept
and grew and somehow appeared to thrive in this city,
the landscape that appeared cauterized and broken,
with these strange Dr. Seuss–like plants that towered
over the piles of rotting flesh.

It's worth the walk, he proclaimed with a grin. *Don't
worry, if you get tired, I can carry you.*

The offer had probably seemed romantic and
thoughtful at the time, but in retrospect, she had been

supremely uncomfortable with the idea, and though her feet ached she didn't want to impose, and for most of the walk she had felt like she was on the verge of fainting, the corners of her vision slowly blurring and darkening and her breaths feeling more shallow as they went on.

Are you feeling all right? he had asked.

Just the smell, probably, it's nothing. I'll feel better when we get there.

She had believed in his sincerity, in his care *for* her, not *about* her, and again, in retrospect, in every manner at which he had convinced her he was *accommodating*, she could see now that he had only been trying to lift up himself.

Wow, I'm so lucky to be on a date with a beautiful, intelligent woman like you.

You're the only published writer I know.

No one else sees how beautiful you are.

It went on like this. Of course she was flattered. Of course she liked the compliments. But in retrospect, every compliment about her had still centered around him, had still been about what he was gaining from her, like an appliance, a new toaster oven, but hardly a human being.

The entire time during dinner (she had ordered the birria and he had ordered the enchiladas), she felt a slightly veiled threat of discomfort, and though she felt accommodated by him, there was something about his optimism that bothered her. *He really is a good guy,* she kept telling herself. He had answered so many of her questions correctly, or so it had seemed. But with that past behind her, though she had believed the strange feeling of discomfort had just been an awry sense of unfamiliarity (that is, *her* problem and not *his*), she realized now that the sinister arrogance in his feigned humility, the dangerous violence in his enactment of compassion, and because he had done so much for her (brought her water, turned off the lights, carried her groceries, opened doors, collected her mail, took a photograph of her dog), she had convinced herself that she deserved to be happy, that she deserved someone who would do these things for her, and who else would love her this much? And so, she told him she loved him too.

A few weeks later, she read about a terrible incident in the news where, in a small town very far away, several men had raped a pregnant goat. The goat had died from the trauma soon after. When she read the story, she couldn't breathe, couldn't see more than a few feet past herself, couldn't understand *why*, and as if she had come down with something, started to tremble from extreme cold and then from extreme heat and her vision blurred and her chest tightened and she went to the sink to wash the sweat off her hands but the perspiration only increased and she was trembling so violently, and so she threw herself onto her bed and sobbed into her pillow because she couldn't understand *why* and outside there was a distant cooing that might have meant something on another morning but today she just couldn't understand *why*, and when he had come over, all he could ask was: *What's wrong?* And when she told him, he simply replied, *Well you don't have to worry about it. That's not your burden.* And what she couldn't explain to him was that somehow, she could feel all of the pain, the goat's, everyone's, and as she was paralyzed with grief he simply sat there with a blank stare on his face because he didn't understand *why,* and they were asking the same question about two different but very related events, because as she lay there sobbing he didn't know how to help her because he couldn't understand *why* she so willingly stepped into these roles of suffering and she sobbed and shook and couldn't understand *why* no one else was feeling what she felt, these feelings that she couldn't control, and that was the difference between the two of them, that she wanted to do something in moments like this but because she was trapped by her own anguish, she only knew to despair, and he chose to hide from the atrocities of the world, to ignore them, to simply go on and walk *around* the rotting bodies — how else to get from point A to point B — and he chose not to feel these things because he thought there was a choice, but couldn't understand that for her there was no choice, just the intensity of feeling, and in the end, this was the real distance between the two of them.

As a sort of reactive gesture, she had started to make a list of words to ban, in remembering her encounters with him, certain words would fill her with rage, in particular, she felt the desire to ban the word *just* — that reductive and condescending word that seemed to oversimplify everything, and cringed every time he used it in an attempt to make her feel better, because instead the word's employment would make her feel smaller or somehow wrong; *there is no positive use of the word,* she thought, and she hated the kind of logical thinking it induced.

But instead, she redirected the intensity of her emotions, and in an attempt to reach outward like the creeping tendrils of the pea plant, she combatted the loneliness she might have had in this place by starting a garden, and as she would squat by the plants each morning, time passing on the surface of the soil and her fingers somehow in tune with *that* time rather than her own, she felt somehow grounded in the ground beneath her, somehow less alone, because as she breathed out there among the plants, they were breathing together, and because the growth of the plants signaled a constant becoming, it reminded her of living, and as she tended to the garden everyday, the silence grew within her but now the silence wasn't darkness or pain, but simply the state of being, and she might have learned to listen, sitting there on her knees, eyes pointed downward at the dirt that sprawled out in all directions below her.

33. THE CAT

The eclipse is silent, and though totality only lasts for a few moments, the details continue to fall one after the other around you and it is only because the sun has foreseen the fall. To be a memory and to be alive are one and the same thing, so when we move from here to there, we know that life is a series of breaths: to see a perspective only when the seer and the seen are perfectly aligned, that is, to be in a position to be able to see and to want to see. The humans know that a lunar eclipse occurs only when the sun, earth, and moon are aligned in syzygy, our home planet's shadow creeping across the moon until the moon appears red because our atmosphere acts as a filter for the sun's light, or that during a solar eclipse one should never look directly at the sun, but things aren't so extreme — what will you say to me? — though the spiders may begin to dismantle their webs in the middle of the day and the dog may howl before the rains come, the transition between light and dark is the transition between life and death is the journey of living itself, is this, all of this, that the measure of being worthy of belonging to the land is the measure of sight. We have not arrived yet at the stage of facing each other straight on because there is still that lingering feeling of guilt, but all along you were planning on saying something else. Still, we all are here, watching, judging.

34. THE OLD MAN

It was as surviving a shipwreck, as if he knew exactly
how many days had passed since the ship had run
aground in the storm, but what had been lost was
not a ship, some wooden vessel that would transport
him away from here where he might be able to sit,
legs crossed in the sun, one hand holding a glass of
lemonade and the other an oatmeal cookie, no, he
had lost something far greater, something that felt
like bones cracking, like being torn asunder under a
starry sky, like perhaps his old life was lost forever
and, *Here, I don't know how to go on*, he thought, as if
surveying the island he had washed up on, as if, *This
was the shore where he might die*, and it was hard to know
if this was the very shore he had originally set sail for,
but here he was, grieving the loss of something he
couldn't remember and when he looked out upon the
vast darkness what he saw was the blue sea, just like
in the Emil Nolde painting, thick and blue and green
and dense and swallowing, that sense of gazing for a
long while at something but only the tiniest stirs and
movements that let you know you are not eyeing an
artificial image but the real landscape, just that still,
just there, still, and still, and then something stirred in
his chest, a great and urgent desire to know how to set
sail, that is, he had been fixed at this point for so long
(how long had he been simply standing there on the
shore, soaked through and filthy, the other survivors

asking him more and more specific questions that he couldn't answer, and all he could do was continue to listen, that is, continue to live his life in the way that he had, with so much control over everything around him to make things just so), so that everything had revolved around him, and even when hit by a storm such as this one, he had somehow managed to keep it all in orbit. But he did remember, didn't he? He knew he had to get out, even if he died on the journey (wasn't life just the journey to death anyways?), and he whispered, as if the incantation would make it true: *I'd like to know how to set sail.* There he stood at the edge of his bed, hunched over, his right hand still grasping the mattress for support, outside some kind of maddening squall of birds and dogs subtracting, and he thought for a moment he could feel the slow binding movement of the ground beneath him, a sort of rumbling that vibrated his feet, a tremor that emanated from difference, that is, the difference in remembering and not remembering that had triggered all of it, and the mattress was all he could hold onto to keep himself from shuffling like a crab and because he was tired, he stood still, stood completely still for just a moment longer to open his eyes and see. Wasn't it just the morning, or, was it the feeling of the cold ground on his bare feet that might drive him to insanity?

After a recent accident, the old man had slowly been losing his sense of smell and taste. The injury had mostly affected his nervous system and his sense of balance, but the doctors explained how his ears and nose and brain were all linked, and at first, he took solace in the fact that he was still mobile and would take his evening walks and listen to the birds outside but as his sense of smell and taste faded, so did his connection to food and the memory of his mother and the desire to walk to the grocery store and the usage of his joints and his interest in organizing the spices and his enthusiasm in organizing at all and gradually all the pleasure of chewing food dissipated and because he had to eat but couldn't enjoy it, he started to feel more and more like the food he was chewing inside of his mouth than the chef preparing the food, and he began to have dreams of being diced up and thrown into a boiling pot of broth or being pruned then plucked alive and a giant monster's mouth taking a bite out of his side, and one day he planted two tomato plants on his balcony and it became his morning routine to come outside each morning to check in on the plants, to breathe next to them, to try his best to shield them from the heat but let them absorb some of the sunlight, and he could sense their struggle in the climate and he could only describe it as the feeling of getting close to a fire, or, to a truth, and it was all he could do to prevent himself from drowning in the heat, from simply slipping away into steam, but the tomatoes articulated for him better than anything else what was happening, and each morning he would check to see if the tomatoes had ripened and it was his conviction in the hopelessness of the situation, the hope within the despair, that kept him going, after all, he felt no need to try to explain his own actions to himself but he had made mistakes and he had chosen a certain trajectory that couldn't be undone, and wasn't this the kind of waiting that could lead to something quite extraordinary?

He knew the facts: The tomatoes were not ripening, though day after day he offered his eyes and pruned them and watered them and watched the sun. It was too hot. In these extreme temperatures, the tomatoes wouldn't begin the process of senescence and therefore wouldn't ripen. Senescence was, essentially, the process of getting old. The old man was now old, getting older, and he too, like the plants, was sessile and barely left his apartment. Tomatoes, when ripening, give off ethylene, which induces other nearby fruits to ripen. Smoke also gives off ethylene. Burning almonds give off ethylene. If one were to pick the unripened tomatoes and bring them into the apartment where it was cooler, and expose them to the smoke of burning almonds, senescence could be artificially induced. This is the same process that gives color to autumn foliage, whereby the leaves become bright red or orange or yellow, and then, at their peak of beauty, fall to the ground. The descent that makes it possible for others to ascend. It is possible for anosmic plants that are mutants to lose their ability to sense ethylene, anosmia being the loss of the sense of smell, and the old man, after his accident, was now anosmic, and had therefore lost the ability to smell, which also meant that he had lost the abilities to taste and to maintain balance, and though he couldn't ride a bike anymore, found pleasure in other activities like roasting almonds, letting them burn, watching the smoke, and simply, waiting.

The old man didn't want to be led astray by the facts though, because as he knew, facts often betrayed and deceived and oversimplified things, and he had learned his lesson in the oversimplification and overcontrol of life; he had reached a point where a collective self might strip himself of all of his masks, to show his nakedness and be free of any tethers to the past, but he was not haunted by his past—he had longed to be haunted by her ghost, he would have been less alone—yet he had managed to survive, without the desire to survive he had gone to great lengths to ensure his continuance, and when a man loses his love or the obsession that drives him, and when a man is unable to taste the tomatoes that he grows and eats, there is a slow careening down the side of the mountain, the tumultuous crash that happens in slow-motion, and the arrival at the base of the mountain where a ship has been torn apart by the rocks and there lies the single survivor of the shipwreck, and this is when one understands that no map can show a man his fate, that it is his tether to the unknowable and inexplicable that becomes more important even than love, and when one dead man meets a survivor, not even the narrator can tell which is which.

35. THE PHOTOGRAPHER

He isn't surprised when, on a milder morning, the
air still a bit crisp before the desert heat would hit
its peak and obliterate any hope of a respite from the
oppression of the sun, he finally has a visitor. Upon
hearing a knock at the front door, he gets up out of
bed, half asleep, to answer it. He doesn't ask who's
there—he's too excited about having a visitor—and so
when he swings the door open and sees in front of him
a cat meowing in earnest, he feels the settling of the
predilection and prediction that there was a significant
reason to open the door, a calling perhaps, and yet he
doesn't recognize the cat, which is brown with stripes
and is covered in patches of dried blood and is insisting
with the curvature and weight and movement of its
feline body on getting into the house, and yet he knows
too that he was waiting for a visitor, just not this one
perhaps, and yet, perhaps it doesn't matter the species
so long as he is no longer alone in this miserable place,
perhaps this creature was sent to him from someone,
somewhere. He tries to eliminate the possibilities, that
is, the neighbors are scarce—though he could go door-
to-door as it all looks the same out here and he doesn't
want to get lost, besides he's pretty sure he's never seen
a cat lurking around any of the houses nearby—and
it is too hot for any animal to survive for very long
outside without shade or water, and, as he wonders
if he has left out any options, though in reality he has

already made up his mind, he can feel the cat squeezing past his leg, and as the cat manages to dart past him, it shoots him a look of innocence and runs straight for his bed, curling up in the mass of unmade sheets and dirty laundry, all of which he takes as a cue, *It likes me,* he settles, perhaps with some kind of arrogance but too he knows that animals think with scent and the cat wouldn't have been drawn to the bed if not for his own odor that is permeating through all of it, and thinks the cat must have chosen him for some reason, and mostly he is just glad to not be alone anymore.

The night before, the photographer had been standing outside under the stars, *It's all linked,* he had been thinking, and fancied himself in exile, that romantic gesture of being too transgressive or brilliant for one's time, a kind of titular crowning of simultaneously being "better than" and "not nearly good enough" and "to be erased from history" and "to be memorialized as filth" and so on, when he had seen a large metallic orb in the sky that seemed to simply appear in front of him, hover for a few seconds, then, blink out of existence, the only evidence of it having existed in the afterimage residue of bright spots across his vision—like when staring at the sun or a bright light for too long and the brightness follows even when you avert your eyes— and all he could think was, *I don't think the desert is the place for me.* His skin had been irritated for days, red itchy spots around his armpits and shoulders and sides of his belly, as if he was having an allergic reaction to the entire environment, though it was probably just a combination of a heat rash (the kind that babies often get), and the fact that he had put on a little weight (he never left the house and had gotten into the habit of eating grilled cheese sandwiches and chips all day, and had started to feel his undergarments chafing around all the folds of excess flesh), and now, with this possible sighting of a UFO, and the strange rejection he felt that he somehow hadn't been interesting enough to be abducted, he just thought, *What a broken sky, what a broken world.*

In his strange admiration for order though, he did find it easier to categorize things in the desert. Out here, it was flat, there was hot and cold, and day and night, and life and death, and there seemed, to him, to be very little in-between. Since leaving the city he had finally learned what homesickness was, that is, he was finally discovering that ongoing process of the instability of identity, but this wasn't how he thought of it. He knew that he needed new rituals to create some kind of foundation in this new place, so he turned to food, making it and eating it. He hadn't touched his camera since he had arrived, and spent most of the day looking out the window at the vastness, something oceanic about it all, the ephemeral waves of heat, the uncertain visitations, and every thought a mutation of a previous one, though he could very clearly see why this was the place it would all end, or where it had all started, and though, he thought, some people die many times, he would only need to die once to know what it was all about and then surrender himself over to the cosmos, a gesture of surrender that would become one of remembrance and civility.

The cat, perhaps bored, or perhaps ready to move on, walks back over to the door, scratching at it lightly as an indication to be let out. He doesn't understand what he has done wrong, why it wants to leave, and his most immediate desire is to prevent it from leaving, to keep it here as his companion and with enough time, the cat would learn to love him, though the cat is a cat, and it is autonomous and independent and it came of its own free will and should leave with that same free will intact, he convinces himself, so he opens the door and watches the cat saunter away, dried blood still caked on its fur, some of the blood now staining his sheets and clothes and floor, and he can't help but feel betrayed when he sees, off in the distance, a porch light flicker on, a front door slowly open, a high-pitched voice greeting the cat, and then, the sound of the door shutting.

36. THE WHALES

What is the pattern of predictable sounds that, in its
steadfast refusal to cooperate with its interpreters,
shakes you at your chest, wraps its oral tendrils around
your waist and asks: what do you see in your future?

She was seized by the fullness of survival and as
the last boat sped past, she gritted her teeth and
shouldered her body next to her mother's, seams of
space closed off by flesh, and as the water began to
clear, she was able to see again. She scooted up to look
into her mother's eyes, and the eyes let her know, they
had seen everything they needed to see, or, there had
been nothing to see at all.

They had, in the past days, seen many of their friends
disappear or leave—any insistence on coalition heard
silence—and there were less and less tiny things to
swallow up, less and less places to hide large bodies
from those that lurked in the shadows above the
shadows, so that swimming to the surface to watch
the dust dancing in the sun was no longer a relished
pastime.

Her mother had tried to remain connected with the
others, but they were afraid that her visions had been a
bad omen, that there were so few of them now because
of what she had seen, and that they would better fend
for themselves far away from her connection with the

"kingdom of the dead."

She had now known that before her, there had been
another who had died before even seeing the sky and
that her mother had carried that other upon her back
for several days, the others urging her to *let go*, but how
does one let go of everything, how does one simply
allow for such finality when it is a piece of you that
must be discarded and dropped into the sea. *I won't pass
this on to you, I promise*, her mother would whisper every
evening. Especially on full moons, she would watch
her mother's eyes cloud over, tongue tucked back
and voiceless but water running along the contour
of her massive body, and her mother would hum as
the moonlight rode over her skin and when her eyes
cleared like the water and when she spoke again, it was
always the same.

She didn't want to confess to her mother that she had
started to feel the shudders too, that sometimes, during
the rain storms, she could feel a tiny voice, like a grain
of rice, trying to reach her lips, her resistance making
the voice more insistent, and though she wasn't afraid,
she didn't want to worry her mother; her mother knew
enough death, had enough ghosts following her, hated
knowing the fate and endangerment of their kind but
without the others, could do nothing about it except to
sing, that eerie melody that carried through the water
and over the surface, through air currents and upward
into the atmosphere, the kind of melody that human
composers strove for years to construct, but here, it
poured out of her, more than just a song, but a lament,
an intimate tether to all other forms of life, a resonance
that even the pigeons with their blank stares roosting
on telephone wires would feel but perhaps not be able
to parse, yet this wasn't a sound to be parsed out or
interpreted, it was meant to be heard and received and

felt and transposed into tears or waves or touch: the openness of a broken heart.

Another day ended, and the light bounced off of the trembling surface: two whales bobbing under the starlight.

I like the night up here, she said. *We can see the stars.*

They are not our stars, her mother responded.

Both knew more than they let on to the other, and when the blue of the night finally ran out, they awoke to another boat passing overhead. She didn't know why, but this time, instead of swimming deeper and hiding, she had a feeling penetrate and a voice that ebbed inside her like the tide, and so, in a flurry, she turned to her mother and only whispered, *Don't worry,* as she swam upward to meet the dangling hand slowly slicing the water. The hand, connected to a little girl, was gentle. The little whale jumped up and the girl beamed in excitement, though the girl wasn't alone. There were two men with her, each with various recording devices and other equipment, and they spoke words to each other and the girl responded, and as more lights turned on, the girl leaned into the water, put her hand on the whale again, and said simply, *Don't worry.* The whale bobbed there for a moment longer, the girl's hand still resting gently on her head, and when the girl finally removed her hand, the little whale ducked her head underneath the water and returned to find her mother. That night, the girl and the men could hear the whales singing, *They are singing to save the world, the entire world,* she would say, and the men with their fragile devices and advanced machines would record the music and nod in agreement but say nothing, just nodding from time to time as the songs would create spikes of different heights on their screens, all of the lamentations of two grieving souls seeking intimacy articulated in the rise and fall of jagged black lines, and somewhere out there the whales would swim and sing because they were alone, but with each other, a reminder that loss and exile are linked, and the sound was a way to stay connected with the movement of their bodies through the water and the air and the sky and the tremblings of the earth and the breath of all the living beings, and that night, there were more lights in the sky, even more stars being born, and an unanswerable tether to time.

37. THE TREE

A gnarled, red tree sits, and the night refuses to rain,
but in the morning it rains and some of the others
confuse the passage of years with the birth of stars but
when a man is hung, his body hanging from the branch
of the thick-trunked tree, it is not only the little boy
who screams, then is hushed quickly and told *To be a
man*, and at the bone there are cracklings that become
seams that split and unravel and in these tension areas
new seeds might be planted and the "Keep Out" sign
might be uprooted by the tree's massive roots that
keep growing below the surface and *Bye-bye mother*
a girl screams in her sleep but winds sweep over the
imaginations of the dirt, and even the bones become
dust and even the dust becomes soil and even the tree
becomes a piece of paper disintegrated and when the
body is thrown into the ocean it wrinkles from the salt
and the softness that once was compassion or sadness
becomes the light and when the light meets the water,
we name that history, we name that secretion, we
name that land, and when the moon reaches its fullness
the light is so very bright and we are standing, as if
hypnotized, in the endearing shadow of history, and
though the ocean is very far away, the sky is right
above us and what is more elusive than infinity, what
is more elusive than the very dimension you think
you live in; the woes of repetition, or, the wounded

haunt the space you lie in, and when you realize the smallness of your own impenetrable past, there will be no reckoning, only silence.

38. THE WRITER

Verbs: to grow; to see; to wander; to follow; to tend; to meet; to clash; to reckon with; to reach fullness; to be a moon reaching fullness; to be an ocean; to be an archaic identity; to be in the midst of catastrophe; to be a tree; to be a trembling tree; to keep full speed; to be in love; to be a maddening mystery; to claim the same god; to claim no god; to be alone in the midst of waves; to be a memory; to be mediated by a draft of air in the middle of the woods.

The starting point of infinity is always at the center, everything else expanding outwards from that single point, reaching outwards forever in a tortured desire for intimacy, the reaching for the horizon that can never be reached, both infinity and desire being defined by the untenable distance and intimacy that is a mediation of bodies within the paradoxical retreat, but space is made up of layers, and she has so many memory-chambers dedicated to the imaginings of many deaths (her own and of many others), but in the woods she has become unexpectedly close with a man who is kind, who insists on her independence, and though familiar, she feels indecently close to him sometimes. *Is this what love really is?* she wonders, and works to unlearn some of the survival instincts she can't help but hold on to, that is, she does not need to scream, she does not need to fight agony with more agony, she does not need to maintain a wall, she does not need to be who she thinks she is seen to be, she does not need to get help from the dead, she does not need to be fixed, she does not need to live inside a prison, and she does not need to be right.

She is sitting at the base of a large and wide fig tree, the girth of the tree, its expansive roots, all testament to how things stretch beyond their limit and though she has torn her dress — it snagged on an exposed branch as she paced around the perimeter of the tree looking for a spot to sit down — and she thinks about how although this tree is not marked on any map, its extended survival in this particular point in space makes it a landmark, here the branches that extend and reach toward the sky as if reaching for homeland or ancestors, so that the bark of the tree is already fused with the universe's history and to linger too long in a spot like this might lead to thoughts of suicide, that kind of experience evades the kind of description or narrative that she is used to articulating, but she has found peace with the ephemeral, has found, perhaps, her terrestrial habitat — here even her hair seems to be doing better, its volume communicates something about the state of her body that she is still not prone to hearing well — and this tree, which she couldn't wrap her arms around, its circumference is perhaps the distance of eight of her arm-lengths, even if stretched taut, as if being pulled apart by horses in some primitive torture technique, and though she cannot see the other side of the tree from here nor can she find any line of sight with that part of the tree, she would have to walk several paces just to be able to see that particular spot and verify its existence, she trusts it is there, that though the distance between this point and that point is not easily measurable as any straight line,

it is familiar, close, empowering, the sense that the tree
is still living, growing, becoming, and as she breathes
she can feel the tree breathing too, the quality of breath
here as reverent, almost sacred, she can feel her lungs
fill to capacity with the displacement of mountains and
then she can feel her lungs empty with the transfixion
of a leaf opening in the morning to absorb the sunlight,
and her entire body can feel the rhythm of breathing,
not unlike the ebb and flow of the ocean tide, not
unlike the effects of the moon on all bodies of water,
not unlike the effect of gravity on all kinds of bodies,
and at some point some surveyor looked at a map of
this region and might have thought, *This map is not
complete,* but like a bird that can only see from above,
found that it was inclusive of all the preordained
landmarks and allowed this part of the forest to remain
intact and "unimportant," or, if it was not worth
visiting, it would reach its own demise naturally, and
as she breathes she feels the muffled shrieks move
out of her body with the lightness of words and she
feels cold for a moment but then warm again as she
reexperiences the vicissitudes of the journey that
brought her here, so many nights of crying, so many
nights of feeling and not feeling, so many nights where
she thought of death, and she continues to breathe,
the breathing intensifying all of these memories and
simultaneously converting them, momentarily, into
cacophonous clouds disembarking and dissipating
and being absorbed by the tree, all of the trees and
plants around her, and she sees the abstract, gray and
darkening schedule of her past shift slightly in the
swirling air and here, sitting here, participating in this
intimate communion through air, breathing among the
generative and restorative power of the elements, she
feels the closest thing she's ever felt to *peace,* and the
important thing isn't that she feels calm or hopeful,

the important thing is that she feels a continuance in the development of self and environment, that the slow and creaking ship that gently rocks among the other stranded vessels in the bay, the slow lapping of the waves and the rolling in and out of the thick fog, that there is time for movement and there is time for waiting, and then, there is time itself, and she knows the tree has given her a tremendous gift, that though the nightmarish state of affairs might not be over forever, that isn't the point, but she could attempt now to understand the balance that connected it all together, that the tethers are not anchors that imprisoned or shackled, but rather invisible threads connecting and building intimacy *between* things, and she wonders, what can she offer the tree in return; she doesn't know what she could give as a gift to the tree, this tree that has given her so much already, but, as she imagines the impossible navigation through fog, the dangerous rocks hidden in the shallow depths that beckon and threaten the lives of ships, she realizes that here, she is not out of place, she is rather, very much *in* place, and seeing the rip in her dress she thinks about all of the pain she has been carrying on behalf of all of the dead she has encountered, all of the pain that has been inflicted upon her and all of the pain that she has inflicted upon others, these giant rocks she has refused to unburden herself of, and the kind of sensitivity it has induced in her has helped her to get this far, but too, she can make space now to be open, to allow herself to receive and to love, to build up rather than to destroy, and she thinks, *I will give the tree my pain,* because she knows that the tree will not feel the sensation of her pain and suffering, rather, the tree will know to absorb it, to metabolize it, to turn it into a kind of energy for growth and continuance, and in this way, she too could do something good with her pain, could create a new ceremony to bind herself to the land, to be able to move forward and speculate on a future for herself, that this would be her gift, the possibility and imagination of a future where she, and others, could still thrive and remember, that though the trees are burning and the world is becoming uninhabitable, she can feel more than her own tortured past and trauma but instead a pain that is shared, intimate, and allows for a trajectory for moving forward, and so, she says *Thank you,* and that becomes the tipping point, that feeling of gratitude, a feeling that she has never felt before now.

She gets up and brushes the dirt off her legs gently, and walks home. When she opens the front door, she sees the spot on the opposite wall, that without her glasses on, looks like a spider every time.

39. THE OLD MAN

What his wife's death had ensured was that the old man would become sessile, not unlike a plant, that in the intertwining of love and desire he had found himself stranded in a melancholy bay of craggily rocks, any attempt at escape would be dangerous and risky, though the decision to stay, too, would animate a different kind of chaos.

He hadn't been able to sleep, and when dawn struck with a sort of stupor, he was taken back to a childhood memory where he would sit in a field of grass and mindlessly claw out all of the grass around him, imagining his fingers like one of his yellow toy trucks, an excavator or bulldozer, and he would gleefully dig out patch after patch of grass, and when he was done or was called in by his mother, would leave behind a shredded lawn, the tufts of grass and roots still clinging on to chunks of brown soil. He hadn't really understood that the grass was living at the time, it was connected to the soil, which was dirt, which was dust and small rocks, all of which was dead. It seemed very simple to him then.

His father saw things in convenient categories this way. The family dog only slept outside, as the house was a human abode, and animals were inherently dirty and were meant to live outdoors. Children were under the charge of women only, that is, he wanted nothing to do with raising his son and thus saw all matters of childcare as falling to the woman of the house. He also sought to separate love and desire, and in the pattern of great men who sought control in the attempt to separate the two, put his wife in the role of ordered affection and kept a mistress to supplicate his excessive and carnal desires, all in an attempt to keep things ordered, to maintain control.

When his father died, the old man took an obligatory two days off from school to return home to help his mother, though what he really wanted to do was announce that he was in love (she was an English major, and even as he *did* tell his mother about her, he was remembering the smell of her hair) but before he had even gotten to the part about how they had met in a one-credit seminar, *Plants and Personhood: The Future of Vegetal Thinking,* his mother proclaimed that she did not approve, that he should be focusing on his studies, that an educated woman would only turn out to be trouble, that is, this woman wouldn't be willing to remain in the house to raise his family, and, as his mother saw it, this independent woman was one of the largest threats yet to her son's success and future happiness, so of course, the old man, who was basically a child back then as he remembered it, had tried to resist his feelings, but the only thing he could control was their expression, a temporary fix, the outcome of which was failure, inevitably, because love can't be contained in this way, like pruning and training a plant not to reach for the sun but for its caretaker, and in a matter of weeks, he found himself twisted, doubling back, but the girl had joined a study-abroad program in Hungary from where she sent only a final letter: *Life is a maddening mystery, and I'm sorry I won't be a part of yours. We weren't meant to grow old together, and perhaps I am still too young to think of such things, but your trajectory isn't mine. I have met someone else. I know you will too. The sky is different here. I wish you could see it. I hope you find happiness one day, though, I suspect,*

you will need to disobey your mother to find it. Good-bye. But
the day they had first spoken to each other in the seminar,
the professor had been lecturing about thigmonasty, the
unique responses of plants to touch or vibration. The
professor explained the various tactile stresses a plant might
be exposed to, including wind, rain, snow, insects, and the
possible responses to touch including growth restriction.
He described one study in which a scientist who was
measuring leaf length would go out into the field and
physically measure the leaves each day with a ruler. What
he didn't expect to find out was that the leaves that had
been handled each day turned yellow and eventually died,
and the professor remarked: *They were confronted with the
discovery that one can kill a cocklebur leaf simply by touching
it for a few seconds each day.* He went on about Venus
flytraps, plants whose leaves reacted to fire or burning,
and tree growth patterns in response to wind, and it was
around that time that the girl, who had been sitting next
to the old man, leaned over and whispered, *What about
earthquakes? Do you think there are plants that can sense the
vibrations of earthquakes?* and they sat next to each other
every day after that until one day when she wasn't in class,
and he had been worried and called her, offering her his
lecture notes after she told him her mother had died—it
wasn't unexpected, her mother had been in chemotherapy
for almost a year with little success—but still, he could
hear how different her voice sounded and offered to come
over, and really, talking with her about her mother's
death felt like an absurdity to him, talking about death
in this way at all was an absurd notion, that there was an
attempt to reach some kind of clarity, which could only
be terrifying and unsatisfying, and yet he felt the urge to
comfort her and take care of her, and he very quickly fell
in love with the frail sensitivity with which she lived life, so
that when he received news about his own father's demise
he was more excited to share with his mother his own

newfound happiness, which, as he realized later, had been an entirely naive and ignorant undertaking because life was not this simple, and love, at least for him, would never last.

40. THE BIRDS

There is not much to see in the city after everyone has left, after the city has emptied, except for the birds that linger and keep watch.

One bird sees a tree, and wonders, *What would it be like to be a tree?*

A group of birds stagger toward a pile of sunflower seeds, but upon picking up on the stench of rot, they laugh and stagger off in the opposite direction.

The nights are getting cooler, one bird remarks to another.

Is it getting cold? Another bird asks.

It is difficult to know what happens next, there is little that is written down in the after, that is, we tend to think of deterioration as being so narrative, that it can only become a downward spiral that ends in a final action, then, the curtain, but it is possible that the birds become novelists, their minds approximating the various characters that inhabited these spaces that have emptied, but will not remain that way—nothing is forever, nothing is so linear—and the birds write about the humans that lived with such obscure clarity that they could build automobiles and great cities and make beautiful art but could not see what *they* were made out of or how they were destroying themselves so calmly, so frantically, so anonymously, that the oblivion doesn't end with them — *how arrogant they were!* the birds exclaim — *but they are but a single chapter in the essential project of unknowing.*

In a famous science-fiction novel, written by a now-forgotten bird novelist, the author allegorizes the humans as fish and writes about a world in which we see what it might mean for an entire culture to be crowd-sourced, to have all of history be about themselves.

Let it all end the way it once began, with an opening of eyes and demonstration of brilliance, they justify, and from the created framework of linear time, there exists a planet of fish that have created the ideas of success and failure, of decision and indecision, of cause and effect, all of these ideas tied to the belief in linear time, all of this to learn speed and efficiency, all of this to *solve* and *resolve* and to see finality as an answer that supports the polarization of above water, below water, good and evil, right and wrong, encompassed in a watery center, a world in which its beings learn to speculate based on the past, to see the future as having an origin point, to create goals in order to achieve and to continue swimming, perhaps in patterns, though it may be seen that the recognition of patterns itself is not the only way to assess life.

41. THE DEATH

An environmental extreme is the threshold of all that
has ended and all that has yet to begin. That is, in
imagining a death, your death, her death, my death,
one does not expect the death to be so much more than
just the death itself, because as a series of movements,
the dismantling that a death becomes, the dismantling
of a person, of a body, of an identity, that kind of
reiteration of certain elements opens out into a certain
multiplicity, or, one comes to understand that there
is only one death but also there are many, and they
can all be imagined but the question is which of those
to follow through on, or, in the end, it's important
to remember that everything we know about the
universe, everything we take as certain and true, that it
is important to remember that there is always another
way to explain it all, to see all of the same things as
we do from another vantage point, to arrive at the
same point in space via completely different means, or,
which death is the one that really matters?

It is possible to be the kind of person who idly waits
for death, the lines of the apartment framing and
reframing the deliberation of footsteps, the deliberation
of the supposed sincerity of the bearings that conspire.
There are many sides to every argument. Night and

day do not always make a legitimate composition,
and so the trees that exist side by side exist as bodies
exist, that is, until they start to fall, one by one, and the
question asked isn't the question answered, and as one
smells the rot and deterioration, he might understand
that all transformation is the certainty of death, that in
the realm of synonyms, like death and decay, or illness
and disease, perhaps the two most closely linked are
living and dying, that this is redundant, that this too, is
a rationalization of sunset and sunrise, a specialization
of regret and existence.

It is possible to be the kind of person that always
gets what she wants, that the constancy of size and
movement always work toward achieving an end,
and the impossible boundaries of death are simply
encompassed in linguistic description, that objects
that exist side by side or whose parts coexist are called
bodies, and objects that succeed one another or whose
parts succeed one another in time are actions, and
consequently actions are the subject of description,
and in all this a nostalgia for yesterday because, as she
knows, criminality is relative, and so the ethical order
which so many hold on to is simply another system of
categorization that fails to take into account the kinds
of attachments that really matter.

The hope is that in imagining a death, one might
be able to lose parts of her body without losing her
integrity, that she can resist personhood in the way
that the trees resist personhood in the way that they
are inexorable and necessarily people, or, what is
sacrificed in the name of survival, or, what is lost when
one gains the strength to survive?

42. THE PHOTOGRAPHER

At the precise moment that the photographer is
contemplating the question of happiness — that is,
what does it mean to be happy, that age-old question
that many in his position have spent countless hours
contemplating, going back and forth between the
nature of existence itself, and what role something
like happiness has in the face of survival, questions
of whether happiness is necessary to being human,
whether it is something to strive for (is it, in fact the
ultimate achievement, the ultimate goal of life), or
whether it is a privilege (that it may work like leisure,
that is, only when a person has attained a certain
amount of financial security might they have access
to the abstract notion of *leisure time* that consequently
unlocks access to things like *hobbies* and *philosophy*
and the time to contemplate questions such as this)
but he felt pretty certain happiness was something all
people could have access to, that it wasn't tied to any
hegemonic condition of humanity and that it could
live outside the social and economic hierarchies that
limited people in other ways, and, of course, he had
known many poor people who had been happy, but,
was there a distinction between being happy and
content, was one a more permanent state of existence
and the other a fleeting emotion to be treasured? — he
feels the hot, dead air building up around his body
and hears some kind of loud commotion happening

outside, and as he has no friends and hardly has what
might be categorized as neighbors in this tortured
landscape of sand and heat, but he is curious and so
opens the door to step out into the even deader air,
that kind of dry heat that builds up into a thin but
heavy density, like the air that might come out of an
old and musty hair dryer but without the movement,
without any breeze, just the stagnant and staggering
force of an angry calefaction from hell, and just a little
ways down the road (if he had still been in the city,
he might have said about a block away), he sees a
group of young men, maybe only a little bit younger
than him, or about the same age, and he hears them
hollering and whooping, most of them are shirtless
probably as a consequence of the climate, and then,
when hearing the kind of manic shriek that one only
hears in their nightmares realizes that at the center
of the circle there is the cat, the very same cat that
had visited him a few days earlier and who he had
believed he had developed a special bond with, only to
have been disappointed once again by the realization
that he had just been one of many, that he wasn't any
special person to this animal, just another human, and
because he could only remember the viciousness with
which his grandmother had treated him before she
had passed, that recognition of simply being a human
among many other humans had not been enough for
him, and as the men continue to whoop, he sees one
of them throw an empty beer bottle at the cat who
shrieks again and manages to dodge the bottle but is
hit by some of the shards of glass as it shatters just a
few feet from its body, and even from this distance
the photographer can see that the cat is trapped and
terrified and already somewhat bloodied (who knows
how long this has been going on), and then sees one of
the guys approach slowly with something in his hand,

perhaps with a smile on his face, and he approaches
with the posture of someone who might help; the cat
seems to believe this gesture as well and hesitantly
but slowly angles its body in the direction of the man
who has lowered his head to appear smaller, friendlier,
more approachable, and as the cat curiously casts
his head closer to the approaching hand, another
guy quickly approaches from behind and slips a rope
around the cat's head, and before the cat even has a
chance to glimpse what is in the first man's hand, is
yanked back suddenly, the rope like a noose around
its head, and as the men all revel in the success of
their capture, continue to shout and yell, and as one of
the fellows ties the other end of the rope to the back
of a bicycle, the others continue to laugh and taunt
the cat, as if they can't hear the aghast sounds of the
poor creature, the screams that hardly sound as if
they are coming from an animal at all, almost like a
child screaming while witnessing the brutal murder of
his own parents, and the photographer stands there
paralyzed and stunned (*It's all happening so fast,* he
justifies to himself), and then, one of the members of
the group hops onto the bike and starts pedaling faster
and faster in circles around the other men as they all
continue to cheer and laugh, the cat's helpless body
dragged behind, and the photographer can barely
make out the outline of the cat in all the dust that is
being kicked up behind the wheels and he can sense
the pain of the animal, how it is probably struggling to
get free, to escape the cruel and wicked trap of these
humans, and the photographer can only remember the
jealousy he felt when he had watched the cat leave, and
though he feels the pain rising in his chest, he thinks to
himself silently, *It's not my cat,* and as he feels the pangs
in his heart, he thinks, *He's not even my friend,* and as
he continues to watch, the cat's body still unmoving, *I*

don't owe him anything, and as the dust begins to settle, the bike still slowly moving around with just a limp body dragged in circles behind the spinning wheels, he insists to himself, *It's not my responsibility,* and when the bike finally stops he can see the dust caked over the bloody body, and because he has successfully convinced himself that what he has witnessed was none of his concern, he returns inside and quickly removes the image of the cat from his memory, and instead of returning to his chain of thought around the notion of happiness (he had absolved himself from having any role in the situation but still felt that returning to that previous series of thoughts was somewhat morbid and unsympathetic), he instead imagines himself walking on a frozen surface back to his chair, an attempt at trying to feel cooler in the heat, and thinks about the mechanisms of power, the ways in which people can convince others to do things, to harm others or even themselves, and the various ways in which one might be manipulated emotionally, and he can understand that power is simply an accumulation of all the hierarchies humans have created via our senses (sight, hearing, smell) and systems of articulation (language), and because we insist on an increased simultaneity of narratives we don't know how to negotiate each of these hierarchies, or know that we can in the first place, and therefore have become complacent to this simplification of reality, that this is really the root of hegemony, and that though simultaneity also offers choice (we look at each other, we can move past looking, we can choose what to look at and what to see and how we want to be in the world), he still cannot get the image of the cat out of his mind, and in the failure to distract himself he has appropriately carved out the foundation for some kind of insight into his own trauma perhaps, has allowed for some kind of opening back into his own past and how that may have influenced future actions, but he can convince himself of anything, and has already convinced himself of his status as a survivor, the circumstances surrounding his past have been shirked off and discarded and so here he is, improved and strong and conscious and compassionate, and the invention of such an identity only relies on the strength of his belief and the gestures with which he follows through with and so he thinks, he will write her a letter, will apologize, though he still feels she has wronged *him*, he would, in fact, take the higher road and assume responsibility in order for her to understand how much he loves her and that this is, in fact, a small sacrifice in the trajectory to finding happiness.

43. THE DREAM

In a dream there is a girl who encounters a large bear
in the woods, and the bear, in its insistence at being
a bear, stands tall and growls menacingly to warn
the girl to turn back and go home, and the girl, in its
insistence at being a girl who still falls asleep gripping
her teddy bear tightly moves closer, wondering how
soft the bear's fur might be, and the bear, though
confused but gripped with his own intentions and
narrative, bears his teeth and the girl runs forward
squealing and giggling and wraps her arms around one
of the bear's legs and feels the rough fur on her cheek
and a strange but not unfamiliar odor emanating from
his body and the bear slowly leans down and strikes
the girl—who is still hugging him tightly—with his
claws and discards the little body into the river where
it stains the surrounding water red and redder and
what the girl had thought to herself just before she was
killed was how much coarser the fur had felt than she
had expected but still the warmth was comforting and
that she could have fallen asleep right then and there—

44. THE FOREST

The leaves are small and the growth happens discreetly
but each individual plant becomes a little *more* each
day, entanglement and exchange being the primal and
primary desire; that is, this is a communion of sorts,
as well as a cautionary tale, that the distance between
bodies can't ever be measured effectively if *distance*
remains a word—a vehicle—for the articulation of
separateness or absence, and that, in a place where the
interplays between life and death are never forgotten,
rather, the persistence of darkness is not something to
flee from, than one might simply sit under a tree after
it rains, lingering with the petrichor and trying not to
destroy too much.

45. THE BREATH

Imagine, after death, the kind of breath that might finally be possible.

Why is survival always a matter of struggle?

In the breath, there is the acknowledgement that we are all a part of the same sphere of life, not the division of natural and human or plant and animal, but that the breath itself can decategorize the arbitrary categories of living, because whether we ask them to or not, plants breathe for all of us, and don't ask of us anything in return.

46. THE WRITER

The clock on the wall gently ticks as a reminder of continuance, and as she stands in the doorway, the window open and a slight breeze blowing the curtains from side to side, she sees laid out on the kitchen counter the cedar needles and leaves and bark she had harvested the previous day, after, in a dream, the recipe for the cedar tea that her mother had made for her as a child had resurfaced serendipitously, and though she knows that out here, in this quiet place, she is learning slowly, but that also, it is far more important to learn that there is something *yet* to learn in the first place, and in the woods among the trees there is indeed still *so much* yet to learn, and as she sets out on her task in preparing the bark, she remembers learning the various parts of speech, particularly, the difference between nouns and verbs, and after school explaining to her mother what she had learned, that nouns were people, places, or things and that verbs were actions — but as she grew older these distinctions had become murkier, that is, *why were people and things in separate categories anyway? and why were verbs so much about movement or things happening?* she would wonder, and as she saw the distinctions to be limiting, would attempt to reorient these categories of existence in her writing exercises at school, writing, for example, *Today is excited to be Friday,* and her teacher would correct her and explain that one couldn't personify *today* and that it would be simpler and more correct to write, *I am excited that today is Friday,* but the writer would explain that there was an important difference in declaring that it *was* Friday, as a fact, thus dismissing the unique state of existence of Today *being* Friday, and that it wasn't her own excitement she wanted to convey in the sentence, but time itself, that the day, as a durational period of time existed in a state of *being* Friday for only a temporary feeling of time before it would then become Saturday, and this wasn't so different from a human feeling a particular emotion like sadness for a period of time, after which they might become more hopeful, but the teacher, without any adequate explanation, simply stated she couldn't write sentences that way, that it just wasn't the way language worked, and so the writer realizes that she is, in some ways, recovering from the placement of these kinds of restrictions on her relationship with the world, that is, though her teacher had simply seen language as a logical system with certain rules to be followed, she had felt language as an extension of her own ability to see and feel and to be able to articulate those experiences somehow with others, and now, with the breeze blowing in and causing some of her hair to fall over her face, she blows out of the side of her mouth in an attempt to blow her hair out of her face, her hands still preoccupied with the cedar, and she can hear the clock ticking but not much else, not even the birds, and because she is still recovering from the effects of the accumulation of all of the experiences in her life, these great and joyous and traumatic and mysterious experiences, she finds that she can't locate the right words in this moment to articulate the imagining of a future that is her own, that is not the future in which she is dead already, or even dying, but a future in which she is older than she is now and no longer imagines what a future death would

look like, but simply waits, the kind of waiting that is
steadfast and a stand in the name of life itself, and feels
a little shaken, not greatly but just a little because she
feels for a moment not herself, and her only excuse for
feeling this way is that she has never made this tea by
herself before and perhaps there is some kind of
unconscious nostalgia or connection to her mother that
has taken over her body, but in honesty, she *does* feel
herself, but also somehow a future ghost of who she
might be if she continues to keep arriving at this point,
that is, the point of continuing to *want* to become,
rather than the inclination to give into the depths of
finality, and as she imagines what she might look like
as an older woman (she wonders how much she
resembles her mother, how much she *will* resemble her
mother), and as she continues to stand there in this
strange, transitional state, her hands still working as if
the recipe has resurfaced inside the physical memory of
her body, her new lover walks in and embraces her
from behind, smiling, and she is surprised at his easy
affection, and he leaves her to what she is doing (he
believes in the possibility of simultaneous
codependency and independence, and until she had
met him, she had forgotten what peace with another
person might feel like, the kind of care for another
being that doesn't conflict with one's own right to exist,
and one night when she had confided in him about her
own painful past and her desire to move past these
tethers, not to forget them or to make them disappear
but to move forward in a way that felt compassionate
toward both herself and to those around her, and he
had told her that he loved her and she had found it
easy to say she loved him too and he had asked if he
could continue to love her and she had replied that it
wasn't her right to give that kind of permission and he
had said that the permission she would grant would be

in terms of the kind of proximity that she wanted to put between them and she had nodded genuinely, somehow both afraid and hopeful for everything that lay in store for her) and she tries to listen to her heart, how it is beating, why this strange feeling as if she is somehow hovering ever so slightly above her body looking down at herself busily preparing tea, and she remembers the many moments in which she felt she absolutely had to die because life had somehow become too much or too little or she had wanted, in some way, to face a different kind of eternity, but that now she could see so much more in even the air, all of the space that emanated around her and from her, moving in all directions, not the tortured landscape of the city (but not the city itself, just her involvement and interpretation of it as a ruined place), and she could feel somehow a future self emanating from one of those directions, she didn't know how to explain clearly, even to herself that she wasn't simply imagining with some kind of easy curiosity or wonderment at what she would be like in thirty years, but that she somehow was embodying a kind of *remembering* of the possibility of a future, that feeling of how it would be *to be* that future self, and from that point in an imagined but possible future, not so far from death but not under the grip of its ominous shadow, she saw the possibility of family, of knowing what it might mean to create life and to see it grow, and then to understand the kind of loss that parents might feel when they outlive their own children, and she saw the possibility of the admiration of birds, perhaps a significant or sentimental image of one hanging on the wall, and she saw the possibility of numerous trips to various destinations around the world, the piecing together of the acceptance of her own self through the understanding of physical distance, and she saw the possibility of assembling the kind of story that might hold all of these experiences simultaneously, the book being extraordinary and moving and received by numerous others in a way that might finally convince her that writing really could be beautiful and compulsive, even just for herself, and she saw the possibility of a kind of arrival in a place where there might be a plaque on a wall, her fingers running over the etched drawings and letters, a kind of imprecise memorial to her own loyal and resolute dog, the one life that had made the most difference to her when it had mattered, though she would not know for some time just how much he had done for her, and then, she remembered saying good-bye to a friend one afternoon in a café who was flying across the world the next day in order to pursue an alternate treatment to the aggressive cancer that was killing her, and she remembered reading about the final collapse of her childhood city in the desert, a great earthquake swallowing up what had remained of the great metropolis and the rest falling into the sea, and she remembered when the government had issued a state of emergency, decades before, and how, like the wind, things had continued the way they had for some time, and she remembered when a fire had broken out in the forest and had destroyed thousands of acres of trees and her cabin in the woods and the garden she had cultivated for years, and she remembered the countless times she had imagined that it was the end, and all of the times she had managed on, and she remembered, once on a plane, the moment the plane began to descend beneath the clouds and one moment she could see the brightly lit and expanding city unfolding out below her, a brilliant landscape of lights and systemized movement, but then a moment later, the plane began to dip below the clouds, and in that stretched-out moment of time, it felt as if everything slowed down and expanded around her, crushing her with the expanded space, the suffocating largeness of it all, the claustrophobic realization of space and height and her place on that plane, with all the people sitting there in their seats around her, her eyes locked onto the dismal and thick, thick white outside the window, looming and full, and a momentary lapse in sight that was, in its own way a kind of opening of vision, a revelation, and when the apocalyptic moment passed and the city burst forth again beneath the clouds and the familiar brightness reminded her that no time had passed at all, not really, but also knowing that she had lived an eternal purgatory in that moment, as if alone and shivering and quivering in the corner of a tiled shower, the water pouring down and she a body that could only shake and absorb the water through her skin as the tears rolled out of her eyes, and when her feet were on the ground again, she only thought of the immensity and magnificence of the sky.

NOTES

CHAPTER 1

page 8   Reference to *the crack* in Amy Pond's wall, *Doctor Who,* (BBC TV series).

CHAPTER 4

page 33   "It's a far, far better thing I do than I have ever done; it is a far, far better rest that I go to than I have ever known." Charles Dickens, *A Tale of Two Cities.*

CHAPTER 5

page 36-37   Reference to the definition of the Korean concept of *han* as defined by Suh Nam-dong, quoted in *Wikipedia* entry on *Han (Cultural).*

CHAPTER 6

page 43   Reference to scene in *Harakiri* (Dir. Masaki Kobayashi, 1962).

CHAPTER 10

page 74   "He had read a book on Scholastic philosophy and had come across the term *aevum. . . .*" Reference from *Wikipedia* entry on *aevum.*

page 75-76   "One scholar had written, *Aevum* is the proper sphere of every created spirit. . . ." from *Theology and Sanity* by Frank Sheed (Ignatius Press, 1993), 91, quoted in *Wikipedia* entry on *aevum.*

CHAPTER 15

page 99   Reference to the lyrics of "Love Can

Hold It All" from *Nashville* (TV Series)
Season 6, Episode 12).

CHAPTER 17

page 112
"Inventing a new science, nauscopy, [Bottineau's] ability to see traveling ships. . . ." Reference from "Nauscopy: The Art of Detecting Ships on the Horizon at Impossible Distances," *Faena: Aleph,* https://www.faena.com/aleph/nauscopy-the-art-of-detecting-ships-on-the-horizon-at-impossible-distances

CHAPTER 18

page 118
"Every corner beneath the Blue Sky is ours for the taking . . ." Referenced from *Marco Polo* (TV series), Season 1, Episode 2, 2014.

CHAPTER 30

page 165
"Eternity, whose shredded copy is time . . ." Jorge Luis Borges, "A History of Eternity," *Selected Non-Fictions,* edited by Eliot Weinberger (Viking, 1999), 128.

CHAPTER 34

page 176
Reference to the painting *Blue Sea* by Emil Nolde (1918).

CHAPTER 39

page 198
"They were confronted with the discovery that one can kill a cocklebur leaf simply by touching it for a few seconds each day." Referenced from study by Frank Salisbury in *What a Plant Knows: A Field Guide to the Senses* by Daniel Chamovitz (Scientific American / Farrar, Straus and Giroux, LLC, 2012).

ACKNOWLEDGMENTS

A debt of gratitude for inspiration and telepathic channeling to Mr. Bungie the cat.

Much is owed to the music of Russian Circles, the soundtrack to which the entirety of this novel was written and edited.

Through osmosis and absorption, I owe much to the ideas, thinkings, and writings of Etel Adnan, Bayo Akomolafe, Grace M. Cho, Emanuele Coccia, Mahmoud Darwish, Vincianne Despret, Charles Foster, Renee Gladman, Kim Hyesoon, Luce Irigaray, William James, Han Kang, Bhanu Kapil, Robin Wall Kimmerer, Eduardo Kohn, and László Krasznahorkai, Suzanne Simard, Béla Tarr, Anna Lowenhaupt Tsing, Thich Nhat Hanh.

I am fortunate to have so many brilliant minds and generous friends in my life, who read early versions of this work, who encouraged and supported me, who helped in this process in a myriad of ways: Harold Abramowitz, Amanda Ackerman, Will Alexander, Kimberly Alidio, Eddy Alvarez, Rosemary Beam & my fellow Rising Fire Healers, Blake Butler, Teresa Carmody, Jessie Carver, Richard Chiem, Chiwan Choi, Nicole Chung, Gabrielle Civil, Brian Evenson, Brenda Iijima, Porochista Khakpour, Sueyeun Juliette Lee, Marie Lo, Thirii Myo Kyaw Myint, Gabriela Torres Olivares, Jay Ponteri, Andrea Quaid, Nancy Romero, Zoë Ruiz, Michael Seidlinger, Brandon Shimoda, Julian Smith-Newman, Anna Joy Springer, Dennis James Sweeney, Jon Wagner, Jared Woodland, Lidia Yuknavitch, Leni Zumas, Corporeal Writing, and the PDX WOC Writing Group.

Special acknowledgmentsto: the pigeons of Tijuana, Mexico; the moss living in the Drift Creek Wilderness of

Oregon; and Tahlequah (also known as J35), member of the Southern Resident Killer Whales residing in the northwestern Pacific Ocean.

So many thanks to Katie Jean Shinkle, J. Bruce Fuller, PJ Carlisle, and Texas Review Press.

Thank you to my dearest dears: my parents, my sister Emily, Josh, my mooshes Benny & Maggie, and to all the mooshes everywhere.

Earlier versions / excerpts have previously appeared in: *Calaveras Station Literary Journal, Catapult, Cosmonauts Avenue, Diagram, Dum Dum Zine, Enclave, Entropy, Heavy Feather Review, Kithe, Medium, Moss, Old Pal, Peach Mag, Pulpmouth, South Dakota Review, Talking Book Vol. 1 Brooklyn, Weird Sister, Wildness, & WOHO Lit.*

JANICE LEE is a Korean-American writer, editor, publisher, and shamanic healer. She is the author of seven books of fiction, nonfiction, and poetry, including *The Sky Isn't Blue* (Civil Coping Mechanisms, 2016) and *Separation Anxiety* (CLASH Books, forthcoming 2022). She writes about interspecies communication, plants and personhood, the filmic long take, slowness, the apocalypse, architectural spaces, plant and animal medicine, inherited trauma, and the concept of han in Korean culture, and asks the question, How do we hold space open while maintaining intimacy? She is founder and Executive Editor of *Entropy*, co-publisher at Civil Coping Mechanisms, co-founder of The Accomplices LLC, and Assistant Professor of Creative Writing at Portland State University.

Website: http://janicel.com
Twitter/Instagram: @diddioz